What I Hate About You

JESSICA MADDEN

*For Simple Plan, for being the band who always got me
through everything, and helped me to know where I belong*

*And also to my high school friend, Jamie-Lee, for being that
friend who was always there*

Chapter 1

I have hated Simon McGuire ever since Year Seven. I hated him even more when he started dating my twin sister, Lindsay.

Today he was just asking to be murdered. As I reverse park into a space outside Wakefield High, the stupid jerk cuts into it. Lucky for both of us, I slammed on my brakes, preventing our cars from hitting one another.

"Oh, for crying out loud, you stupid jerk!" I cry out, slamming my palm down on the horn in annoyance.

I sit there for a moment, watching Simon instead of moving along, twisting the colourful silicone bracelets around my wrists. This causes the cars behind me to honk their horns in return, telling me to move on. I ignore them, not caring if I cause a traffic jam. Can I kill Simon before I do anything else? The guy must seriously have a death wish for cutting in front of me like that.

Lindsay sits beside me in the passenger seat, letting out a heavy sigh. I do not understand why she is dating that creep. What she sees in him is beyond me. "Alex, please do not do this right now."

I ignore her. Sometimes I wonder why we are even twins. We may be identical with matching medium-length brown hair and green eyes, but we have nothing in common. Some people have trouble telling us apart, even though there are ways of knowing who is who. Like for insistent, I have a purple streak in my hair, while Lindsay recently got her nose pierced. How can it be so difficult to tell us apart?

Cars soon overtook me as I continued to sit there, watching Simon's every move through my rear view mirror. Lindsay sinks down in her seat, hiding her face in embarrassment.

I drum my fingers on the steering wheel, waiting impatiently for Simon to get his ass out of the car. The longer I wait for him, the angrier I feel, which makes me want to get out of this car and strangle him. Sighing, I go back to twisting the silicone bracelets on my wrists.

He takes at least five minutes to emerge from his car. It's like he is taking his sweet time just to piss me off.

He strolls over to the car, leaning on the passenger-side door, greeting my sister with a kiss. I grab the back of my sister's shirt and jerk her away from Simon. She scolds me, claiming I was hurting her.

"You jerk," I say directly at Simon, ignoring Lindsay's complaints. "Don't you have any idea what an idiot you were back there? You're so damn lucky that I slammed my brakes in time!"

"What's the matter, Alex?" Simon says with a cocky smile. "Are you upset that I stole your parking spot?" He put his upper lip out as if he were about to cry. "I'm sorry, but I didn't know that parking space meant so much to you."

"It's the way you stole it! Didn't you see me reversing into it?"

Lindsay sighs. "Just leave it, Alex. Nothing bad happened, so why do you need to get so upset?"

I clench my jaw as I stare back at my sister. Doesn't she know the damage to the car that Simon would have caused if he had crashed into me? Since neither Lindsay nor I have jobs, Mum would have to pay for the damage, and that will cost her heaps!

"Where did you get your licence from?" I ask Simon. "Was it from the back of a cereal box? It's like you don't even know the road rules."

"I got it at the same place you got yours," he speaks with a sarcastic tone.

I frown at him. "You drive like an absolute maniac! You're going to end up in a ditch somewhere!"

Simon places his hand over his chest. "Why, Alex, I didn't know you cared."

I narrow my eyes at him. I hope he winds up dead the next time he drives his car like a maniac. He better not have Lindsay in the car with him when he does.

Lindsay rolls her eyes rather than saying anything. I know she will kill me later for the way I'm speaking to her boyfriend. She is going to stick up for Simon, and not even care what I have to say about him endangering our lives. I may have prevented an accident this time, but what would have happened if he really collided with us? Knowing my luck, Lindsay will blame me for my careless driving, not wanting to look at the fact that it's actually her boyfriend's fault. I have never had an accident since I'd gotten my licence almost a year ago, and I wasn't about to have one with this jerk.

Simon ignores the death stare I'm giving him and turns to my sister. He places a hand on my sister's cheek and kisses her roughly. It makes my stomach churn watching them make out in my car. I watch Simon's every move, his hands all over her, as if I am not here.

He pulls away from my sister and looks up at me, smirking. "Catch you later, Alex."

My brow furrows when I look at him.

Simon turns to my sister. "Linds, are you coming?"

Lindsay smiles brightly. "Yeah, I'm coming."

I squint at her. I watch as my sister unbuckles her seat belt, reaching for her bag from the back seat. Just as she opens the door, I grab the back of her shirt before she has time to get out. I know she will start an argument with me for not allowing her to go out with Simon. I can't control her when she gets out, but as long as she is in this vehicle with me, she is not going anywhere with that creep. Lindsay shouldn't even be hanging out with him. He is not even worth being with.

She lets out a frustrated sigh. "Let go of me, Alex."

"You are not getting out of this car until I say you can."

"You can't tell me what to do!"

She glances at me, seeing the death stare I am giving her. Lindsay never liked me telling her what to do. She rolls her eyes and tells Simon she will meet up with him later. He is about to lean over to kiss her again, but I yank on her shirt hard, pulling her towards me so Simon couldn't put his filthy lips on her. It makes no difference to me if they are dating. I don't want him coming anywhere near my sister. I'm sure she could date someone better than someone who isn't a jerk.

Lindsay buckles her seat belt, crossing her arms across her chest. She mumbles "bitch" softly enough for me to still hear.

"I will catch you ladies inside." Simon steps away from the car.

I stick my middle finger up at him. He smirks, returning the gesture before heading towards the entrance of Wakefield High.

I groan. That guy... He's the biggest idiot I have ever met! Thank goodness English is the only class I have with him, and then I don't have to see him throughout the day.

I flick on my indicator, turning back onto the road safely, searching for another parking space.

"I really can't believe you're dating that creep." I shake my head. "What do you even see in him? He is a bad influence on you."

"He is not a bad influence on me, okay?" she argues back. "He is actually a pretty decent guy. Simon is sweet and he cares about me."

I laugh. "Oh, please, Lindsay! The dude only wants to get into your pants."

She rolls her eyes. "It's none of your business what we get up to. Yes, we have had sex, but who are you to tell me I can't? I don't understand why you hate him so much? He did nothing to you."

"Do you seriously have to ask me that question? You know the reason I hate him."

"Just answer the question, Alex."

I sigh. Do I really have to explain it to her? I have countless reasons to dislike Simon McGuire. Dating my sister is one of them. "I hate him for several reasons. At the moment I hate him because he cut in and pulled an idiotic stunt that could have damaged the car and injured us. He knew I was going to park there, but he was too lazy to find his own parking spot."

I see her stare at me from the corner of my eye, like she couldn't decide if I was serious or not. She then rolls her eyes when she realises I am serious. "Oh my gosh, Alex. You're so ridiculous sometimes. Just forget about it, okay?"

"Oh, so you think it would have been okay for him to crash into us?"

"He will not crash into you."

Up ahead, I spot a parking space underneath a tree. I quickly pull into it before someone else has the same idea as me. I am not in the mood to get into another argument this morning over a stupid parking spot.

"I want to know something," Lindsay says as I put the gear into park and switch off the engine. "When are you going to stop hating on everyone? It's really getting old."

Ignoring her, I retrieved my bag from the back seat and exited the car. Lindsay does the same. Our eyes lock over the top of the car. I look away first, pressing the lock button on the remote control. Swinging my bag over my shoulder, I headed towards the school. All I want to do right now is get away from my sister, but I knew that's never going to happen. Avoiding her stupid boyfriend may be easy; Lindsay wasn't. We have roll call first thing in the morning and then English right after. Thankfully, English and P.E. were the only classes we had together. Then we will see each other at home.

Lindsay chases after me. "Hey, where do you think you're going?"

I roll my eyes. "Where do you think I'm going? I'm heading towards the school."

"Are you going to answer my question?"

"I just did. I said I'm heading towards the school."

"No. Not that one. You know which one I'm talking about. God, Alex, do you have to find something wrong with everything? Even a parking spot? Or a question I want to ask you?"

"Why should I answer it when you should already know the answer?"

Lindsay walks in front of me, walking backwards as she faces me. "That's not the answer, Alex."

"Then what is the answer?"

"I don't know." She shrugs, then says, "'Yes, I will stop finding the littlest things to hate on.'"

I chuckle with a smirk. "I'm not going to do that. I really do loathe everyone. You basically know the answer to your own question. I don't need to answer it for you."

"Why do you always avoid this question? I mean, it's not normal for people to just hate everyone or everything."

I stop walking, and she does too, almost tripping over a crack in the path. I wish Lindsay would stop pestering me about why I didn't like anyone or anything. It was my business, not hers. I choose to hate everyone because no one is worth liking over. I mean, you can be nice to people, but they will end up leaving you in the end, act like you never existed and treat you like dirt that they can walk over anytime they want.

"Define normal for me," I say.

Lindsay stands there, unsure how to answer me. Typical. She knows how to throw these annoying and stupid questions at me, but when I ask her something, she can never figure out how to answer.

But just when I think she doesn't answer me, she does. "Well, all I can say is that you don't act like a normal teenager."

I raise an eyebrow at her. Did she seriously think she was better than me? "Oh? And you do?"

She smirks at me. "Of course I do. Teenagers go to parties, have sex, get wasted, have their own mobile phones, and a bunch of other things. All *you've* achieved, by comparison, is getting your driver's licence. What about a phone, Alex? How do you live without one? Or how about you live a little and attend a party, maybe get wasted and hook up with someone?"

I continue to glare at her, wondering how she could even call this normal behaviour. It's not the lifestyle I wanted. What's wrong with being different? Why do I need to be like Lindsay or others?

"Sorry for wanting to be different," I tell her.

Without another word, I hurry away. She continues to chase me, asking me ridiculous questions which I only ignored. I don't need to explain anything to her. I just want to go to school and have others leave me alone.

Chapter 2

There's ten minutes to go until the bell rings. I settle outside the library to relax after everything that happened with Simon before the school day officially starts. I take out my sketchbook and start drawing.

A feeling of relaxation comes over me the instant my pencil touches the paper. Art relaxes me when I have to deal with someone so stupid like Simon McGuire. It's the one activity I enjoy, one that connects me to my dad. He taught me to draw from a young age. When I put that pencil to paper, I forget the world around me as I focus on a drawing.

I get a few minutes of drawing done before the bell rings. I snap my book shut and make my way to roll call. My classmates mingle around the outside of the classroom instead of going in. I enter and take a seat in the back row.

I keep my head down, focusing on my sketch as everyone piles into the classroom and takes their seats, talking about what they did over the weekend or asking others about homework they were supposed to do. I have sketched my father's face so many times over the last six years that I could do it from memory. No one has ever seen my drawings apart from my counsellor. Not even my sister and mother. I refused to allow anyone to see them. They wouldn't understand why I constantly drew pictures of my dad. It's just my way of keeping the memory of him alive since he had walked out on my family.

I keep my eyes on my drawing throughout roll call, not even looking up to see my sister walking into the classroom. For the next fifteen minutes, the only person who speaks is Mr Grey as he calls out our names one by one. I mumble my attendance. The bell soon rings for first period, and I head off to English.

Being the first person to enter the classroom, I take my usual spot in the first row, right in front of my teacher's desk. It's not my choice to sit there. Mrs Callea is the one who seated both me and my sister at the front so she could keep a close eye on us because of our constant bickering. If I had a choice, I would prefer to sit in the back where I can concentrate on drawing and partially listen to whatever the teacher says.

Opening to the page where I last left off in my sketchbook, I continue drawing as the rest of the class arrives in the room. Then I hear her laughter as she walks into the classroom. I glance up from my book to see Lindsay and Simon walking hand in hand into the room.

She kisses him quickly. I roll my eyes at the kiss, then return to my book.

"Lindsay and Simon, I'd appreciate it if you didn't do that in my classroom. Thank you," my teacher admonishes them. I scoff at the thought of my sister getting into trouble. Mrs Callea makes her way over to her desk and sets down her belongings for today's lesson.

Lindsay pulls away from Simon, smiling at him before taking her seat near me, leaving a gap between us. Simon moves to a seat in the back of the classroom. He used to sit with my sister, but our teacher separated them. The two of them never stopped talking and were always interrupting the lesson.

Mrs Callea is not a terrible teacher, but the thing I really hate about her is when she gives us so many assignments at once. She seems to enjoy torturing us with so many of them. It's the same with every other teacher in this school, especially because we are in our final year of high school. Assignments pop up everywhere, one after another, especially just after you have completed one of them. We have only just returned to school a few weeks ago, and the work keeps piling up. It's like teachers think we have nothing better to do with our lives besides schoolwork. To make the workload even worse, we have our half-yearly exams in six weeks.

Mrs Callea stands beside her desk, ready to begin the lesson. I notice she has gotten a haircut over the weekend.

Her strawberry-blonde hair is now level with her ear. She looks ridiculous with that hairstyle. Short hair does not suit her. She should have kept it the way she previously had it when it was past her shoulders.

"Now, I know you all will hate me for doing this," she begins, "but I'm going to get you all to redo the essays I had given you."

The class breaks out in a chorus of groans.

"Hey, groan all you want, but I need you all to keep improving your writing skills, especially with your exams coming up soon. A lot of you did poorly on this essay, and I need you to redo it. My goal is to help you achieve the highest possible grade. Since these essays will not be easy, and you will write more than one. Not just for English, but for other subjects too."

"You can't be serious, Mrs Callea," Simon whines. "Can't you cut us a break? It has been only a week since we returned to school. Why do you have to give us another assignment? We already have assignments for other classes."

Mrs Callea looks in Simon's direction. "I don't know why you're complaining, Simon. You never did the last assignment, which you still have to complete for me. And when I give out this one, I expect you to do it with no excuses about why you couldn't complete it. You don't want to be failing this class, do you? I don't exactly care if you have assessments for other classes or other commitments. You're in my class right now, and I want you to complete the work I provide for you."

Laughter ripples through the class following our teacher's comment. I sigh, already bored, and it has only been a few minutes since class started. Of course, Simon needs to be an idiot and say stupid things to interrupt the class. Sometimes I wish it was just me in the classroom so I don't have to worry about the other students. Maybe I should talk Mum into allowing me to be home schooled for the rest of the year. At least I don't have to worry about anyone interrupting the lesson. I will concentrate on my work better.

"For the next few weeks leading up to your exams, I'm giving you different writing exercises to help improve your skills. You will use different areas of writing, such as essays, creative writing, and poetry. You will need to know these areas, especially when many of you aren't so skilled in this area. Think of this assignment as practice before the real exams so you're able to see what areas you need to improve. I will start you off by redoing the essay I have previously asked you to write."

I tune out as the class groans. Ignoring them all, I continue to draw in my sketchbook.

Mrs Callea resumes. The assignment and what I needed to compose were of no interest to me. I didn't even care if I did poorly on the essay. I'm an artist, not a writer. All I wanted was to draw right now. She explains what she expects us to write in the essay, analysing some poem that she got us to use last time. I find the whole essay unnecessary. Who cares about analysing some stupid poem? I mean, are we even going to be needing to analyse poems or any piece of writing by the time we leave school? Why does an essay have to be so damn perfect to get a good grade? As an artist, I don't think I would need to write an essay for my future career. Maybe if I were to further study art I might, but not when I actually get more involved with the career.

I raise my hand.

Mrs Callea looks my way. I can tell she's fighting the urge to roll her eyes. She never likes it when I ask or give any negative comments on anything that she says during the lesson, especially when it leads to an argument between my sister and me. "Yes, Alex?"

"Is this necessary for us to redo it?" I say, putting down my hand.

"Yes, it is, Alex. It's all part of the curriculum. I would not be getting you guys to redo it if the class didn't do poorly on it the first time."

"Why is it so important for us to learn how to write essays? I mean, once we graduate high school, are we going to be needing to write them in the future? Not unless we go on to further study. But what career would we be needing to write an essay or analyse a poem that was written long before our time?"

Mrs Callea opens her mouth to answer my question, but the door opening and closing interrupts her. Everyone turned in their seats to see who had walked in. I roll my eyes when I see Nathan Bridges with his bag over his shoulder, hurrying into the room. He just had to walk in when Mrs Callea was going to answer my question. He takes the empty seat between Lindsay and me. I sigh in annoyance. Why does he always have to sit between us every lesson? Is this our teacher's way of keeping my sister and me separated during class?

"It's good to have you finally join us, Mr Bridges," Mrs Callea says. "I'm just explaining to the class about redoing your essays that you all didn't get a good grade on. So, what is your excuse for being late this time? Do you have a late note?" Nathan was late for class a couple of days ago. This is his second time being late.

"I'm so sorry, Mrs Callea," he apologises. He pulls a piece of paper from his pocket and hands it to her. She takes it, reading it. "I had trouble getting here this morning. My next-door neighbour threw a party last night. I couldn't get to sleep until two in the morning. I overslept and then woke to find a flat tyre. My dad had to drive me because I didn't have time to change it, and I had already missed the bus. We got caught in traffic along the way."

Mrs Callea looks up and nods. "Okay. Please make sure you come early next time."

Nathan promises he would. He unzips his bag to take out the equipment he needed for the lesson. He glances toward my sister. Lindsay gives him a wave, followed by a flirty smile. Not sure if he returned the smile. He probably did. He gives her a wave and then places his bag on the floor beside his feet. I roll my eyes. Lindsay has nothing better to do than flirt with every guy she comes across. Does she realise her boyfriend is sitting a few rows back? Simon could probably see what she is doing.

"Anyway, as I was saying–" Mrs Callea continued, but I interrupted her. I knew whatever she was going to say would not be about my question. She was going to explain the assessment all over again for Nathan, and I do not want to hear her repeat it the second time just because Nathan came in late.

"Hello, Mrs Callea?" I blurt out rudely without raising my hand. "Aren't you going to answer my question? Why do we even have to write essays? How does it help with our future?"

Mrs Callea sighs with frustration. "Alex, please don't interrupt me when I'm talking. I am going to answer your question. I understand you and everyone hates writing essays, but this is something you have to learn."

I frown. "You didn't answer my question about how it will help with our future?"

"Oh, will you just shut up, Alex?" Lindsay blurts out. "No one wants to hear you complain about what you hate.

Everyone in this room hates writing essays, but no one is making a fuss about it like you. None of us want to rewrite this damn essay."

"Language, Lindsay," Mrs Callea warns her.

I turn to my sister, our green eyes meeting. I shot her a dirty look. Lindsay never knows when to keep her mouth closed or when to stop sticking her nose in other people's business. "Was I talking to you?"

"No, but I'm pretty sure everyone is sick of you complaining about everything that you dislike."

"Shut up and mind your own business, Lindsay."

"Girls," Mrs Callea warns us. "That's quite enough now."

"No," Lindsay spits out, ignoring our teacher. "I don't need to mind my own business."

I laugh derisively. "Yeah, you do. It's none of your concern what I hate."

"Do you realise how pathetic you sound?"

I narrow my eyes at her. I lean forward on Nathan's desk, who is sitting there helplessly, unsure if he should say something or keep out entirely. The best thing he can do is stay out of this. "Say that again."

Lindsay smirks. She leans closer to me until her face almost touches mine. She says the words slowly this time. "You're pathetic."

I yank the loose hair around my sister's shoulders with a hard pull. Lindsay screams as if I had just ripped the roots right out on top of her head. Nathan's eyes widen before he tries to intervene by grabbing my hands to pull me away from my sister, but he only gets knocked in the mouth with my elbow. Lindsay tries to pull my hands away from her, but I don't dare let go. It only makes me pull harder. If she is going to call me names and think she is better than me, then she deserves this treatment.

Our classmates egged us on, enjoying the show we were giving them. Mrs Callea yells at us to stop. When that doesn't work, she gets in between us. I finally let go of my sister's hair. Blood rushes to my head as my teacher steps between us. I momentarily feel lightheaded. Without thinking, I shove my teacher hard, knocking her into her desk behind her. Her eyes widened, startled by my actions. Lindsay doesn't waste any time with our teacher being out of the way by climbing onto the table. She jumps on me. I tumble backwards over my chair, knocking into the table behind me. The edges of the table dig into my lower back, causing sharp pain to shoot up.

Recovering from pushing her, Mrs Callea successfully steps in to break up the fight before someone gets hurt. I was about to pounce on my sister again, wanting to continue what she started, but my teacher wouldn't tolerate my behaviour. She asks Michael Hayworth, the school captain, to hold me back. I jab him in the ribs with one of my elbows as he slips his arms around me. Michael yelps out in pain, but doesn't let go as he holds me back. I scream at him to let me go, but he doesn't until Mrs Callea speaks.

Our teacher scolds us for our behaviour. Rather than sending us to the principal for fighting, she issued us with a lunch detention. She then suggests I move to the back of the classroom, away from my sister. I frown at her. I felt an urge to yell or hurl an object to vent my frustration. Why does Lindsay always get away with everything, and I'm the one people always seem to push away?

"You're moving me?" I protest. "Why don't you move, Lindsay? She is the one who started it!"

"Alex, please," Mrs Callea answers calmly. "I don't want to hear your excuses, so just move and don't make another sound for the rest of the lesson. If you cause any more trouble, I'm afraid I will have to send you to the principal's office."

I glance at my sister. She is smirking, as if she had planned this all along to get me into trouble. A part of me wanted to wipe off her smile, but it would only cause more trouble. I'm sure Mr Matthews doesn't want to see me in his office.

Without another word, I gathered my belongings from the floor. Mrs Callea gets everyone to settle back down so she could continue on with the rest of the lesson. I can feel someone's eyes watching me. I glance over at the person and just as I did; I see Nathan turning away, looking down at his book and pretending to take notes. What is he staring at?

Ignoring the looks everyone was giving me, I storm across the room to an empty seat beside the window.

"Hey, Alex, have you thought of attending anger management?" Simon snickers from the back.

I did everything I could not to walk over to him and punch him in the face. It won't only get me in more trouble, but Lindsay would kill me later for hurting him. Instead, I stick my middle finger at him before dropping my books on the table beside the window with a loud bang. My pencil rattles on the table, dumping my bag on the floor beside me, and I flop myself down.

"Someone is on their period." Simon tries to cover his words with a cough.

"Simon," Mrs Callea scolds. "Enough."

With me now out of the way, Mrs Callea resumes the lesson. She walks over to her desk, continuing to talk about the essay and what she wanted us to include when we rewrite it. If you ask me, rewriting it is just a waste of time. It's not like it will do us any favours for the future.

Lindsay looks my way, giving me a cocky smile and a small wave. I flip my middle finger up at her, then turn away to open the back of my English book, doodling on the last page.

Chapter 3

Even if she doesn't show it, I'm sure Mrs Callea is thankful when the bell rings for second period. She dismisses us, reminding us once again about our stupid essays we need to redo. I couldn't get out of the classroom fast enough, wanting to get as far away as I could from my sister, which will not be easy in this school. Thankfully, she isn't in my next class. I'm sure our teachers would be thankful we are only in two classes together.

As soon as I step out into the corridor, I end up behind my sister, who meets up with her best friend Emilynn outside our classroom. She must have hurried out of the room so quickly that I never saw her leave. Emilynn asks Lindsay what all the screaming coming from our classroom was about. The surrounding classrooms could undoubtedly hear our fight. When we fight, everyone knows about it.

Instead of hurrying past them, I keep a distance behind them, wanting to know what Lindsay has to say about me to Emilynn. She loves bad mouthing about me to her, making me look like the evil twin when she doesn't even look at herself to see what kind of person she is. Neither of them even took notice that I was walking behind them when they started speaking about me.

"What was the fight about this time?" Emilynn wants to know.

Lindsay doesn't waste time telling her everything, immediately making me look like I was the bad guy. Apparently, I was the one who started the fight. Maybe if she had just minded her own business in the first place, I wouldn't have gone off at her.

"Is Nathan in today?" Emilynn asks my sister, switching the topic once Lindsay finished bad mouthing me. "Did you get the chance to ask him out after all the commotion?"

I raise my eyebrow. Was she seriously asking my sister that question, especially when her boyfriend could be nearby and hear their conversation just like I can? Of course, I'm not surprised that Lindsay was trying to get Nathan's attention even when she is already dating someone. She is always flirting with someone. I mean, if she isn't happy with Simon, why doesn't she dump him already?

Lindsay shakes her head. "I haven't talked to him yet. He arrived late today, and then the fight happened shortly afterwards. Besides, even if I got the chance to, I have to make sure Simon doesn't overhear."

"Oh yeah, I forgot he is in the same class."

"I might see if I can talk to him at recess later."

I roll my eyes. These two can't be serious. How can these two talk about asking another guy out when Lindsay is already dating Simon? She's better off breaking up with him than sneaking around with another guy.

Hopefully she dumps Simon so I don't have to see him hanging around my sister all the time.

"You know you wouldn't have to worry about Simon overhearing you if you weren't trying to two-time him for Nathan," I speak up. She is going to kill me for interrupting their conversation, let alone eavesdropping. It was not my fault that I overheard them. I'm sure anyone walking by could also hear.

Maybe Simon is close by to hear it and will break up with my sister.

But the jerk isn't. Lindsay's secret of seeking another guy is safe with her... for now.

The two of them stop walking. I almost crash into the back of them. They turn around, giving me a filthy look for eavesdropping.

"Excuse me, but this is a private conversation," Emilynn spits out. "No one asked you to join in."

I nod, wanting to laugh. "Right, because if this was really a private conversation, then there wouldn't be anyone else around to hear it."

"What is it to you, Alex?" Lindsay snaps at me. "I'm not two-timing Simon."

I smirk. "Yet."

She rolls her eyes, sighing. "I'm trying to find the right moment to ask Nathan out. There is nothing wrong with experimenting with different guys."

Oh God, someone really needs to knock some sense into her. Tell me how we are twins again?

"And you think asking him out while you're with Simon is the right thing to do?!" I ask her, trying to restrain myself from yelling, even though I wanted everyone to hear what I had to say, especially Simon. "It's wrong, Lindsay! You can't date Nathan if you're already dating Simon. Imagine how he will feel if he finds out you're cheating on him. You don't need to date every single guy you come across. Just stick with one guy and stay away from the others."

She stares at me as though she's trying to understand what I'm thinking. I know she doesn't believe a word I'm saying. Or she knows I'm right, but doesn't want to admit it. Lindsay thinks that just because I'm three minutes older than her, I can't tell her what to do. She's a typical younger sibling. She is always thinking that she doesn't have to listen to anything I have to say.

Lindsay narrows her eyes at me. "Who are you to tell me what to do?"

Rather than answering her question, I smirk, almost laughing. "You know, if you don't stop flirting with other guys, I'm going to tell Simon what you have been doing."

My sister stares at me in horror, speechless at what I'm planning to pull. I don't know for sure if I will tell him. Maybe I will, just to piss Lindsay off. She has been dating that idiot for almost a year now, and I have watched her secretly date other guys while she still dated him. How he does not know what she has been doing is beyond me. Someone should tell him what's going on.

Maybe I should find him this instant and tell him. Better yet, I should scream it out in this corridor for everyone to hear. Simon is somewhere in these halls.

"You wouldn't!" Lindsay's voice shakes.

"I will," I say, curling my lips into a sneaky sneer.

Without another word, I push past them and continue down the corridor. I laugh softly to myself. One of these days Lindsay is going to get caught cheating, and I want to be there to laugh in her face, telling her I have told her so.

I make my way to my next class: German.

I see Mr Brown standing at the door to the classroom, his tall figure towering over each student as he greets them in German when they walk in.

He smiles as I approach him, his brown eyes lighting up behind his glasses. "*Guten Morgen*, Alex. *Wie geht's?*"

I don't know why he bothers to greet me. He knows I never respond to him. And why would he care how I feel this morning?

I walk straight past him without a word.

I take my usual seat in the back of the classroom beside the window.

Nathan and his friend Eric Jamieson are the last to arrive into the classroom. Once they take their seats, Mr Brown closes the door and stands at the front of the classroom. He briefly tells us what we are learning this lesson.

Opening up my sketchbook to a clean page, I pick up my pencil and begin sketching the picture I have in mind. I do my best to block out my teacher's voice so I could concentrate on what I'm drawing. German was okay, but I really wasn't in the mood to be learning another language right now.

***

Second period felt like it had gone over fifty minutes before the bell finally rang for recess. As soon as the bell rings, you can literally feel the tension in the classroom that was building up as everyone let out a sigh of relief, finally being able to get out of here. I quickly stuff my equipment into my bag, except for my sketchbook and pencil. I swing the bag over my shoulder, tucking the pencil behind my ear and held my book close to my chest, hurrying out of the classroom. Mr Brown calls out goodbye in German as we walk out, but no one replies.

I push my way past people to the outside, heading towards the shelter area outside the main building. There is one last empty table there, and I quickly hurry over to it before anyone steals it. I unzip my bag and pull out a tuna sandwich. I eat it, continuing the sketch I had started in class.

As I drew, I could feel someone's eyes on me. I glance up and spot Nathan Bridges sitting at a table near me on the right. He is sitting with Eric. As soon as I glance his way, he swiftly turns his attention to Eric, talking about something, acting like he was never looking over at me. I narrow my eyes at him. Why was he staring at me? Can't he find some other girl to stare at? I'm curious about their conversation. Were they talking about me? If they are, I will come over and give them something to talk about. Maybe then Nathan will stop looking over at me.

I look around me to see who or what Nathan was staring at, but with many other students around, I couldn't figure out what it was. Maybe I was just in his line of sight. Or maybe he was watching me. Whatever he was staring at, I really didn't appreciate him watching me.

I turn back to continue on with my drawing. Only I couldn't concentrate on what I was sketching, sensing something over at Eric and Nathan's table. I glance up, and my eyes lock with Nathan's. A strange feeling in my chest forms when our eyes lock. We stare at each other for a brief second before he turns away, saying something to Eric.

I groan. There was no way I was getting any privacy out here with Nathan watching me. I devoured the rest of my sandwich before closing my sketchbook and swinging my bag over my shoulder. Without another look in his direction, I walk the opposite way of his table towards the library. There is no way I'm going to continue sitting out here with that creep watching me. Besides, I enjoy sitting in the library during lunch. It's quiet in there and no one can interrupt you. I spend most of my recess and lunch break in here. I either work on my homework or sketch in my book until my next class starts.

And that's where I stay for the rest of recess until the bell rings.

Chapter 4

Sometimes I wish I were an only child. That way I didn't have to wait around for any siblings after school. Waiting for Lindsay after school so we both could ride home together is the worst. Sometimes I feel she lets me wait for her at the front of school for so long on purpose to annoy me. She spends most of the time talking to Emilynn, flirts with other guys or spends too long saying goodbye to Simon at the front gate. It's like I have nothing else to do for the rest of my afternoon while she makes me wait.

I lean up against the fence, groaning. The bell had rung fifteen minutes ago. It doesn't take long to walk out of the school. She should be out here by now, but she isn't.

After a few minutes of waiting, I spotted her amongst the crowd. She is with that son of a bitch Simon, laughing about something he said.

I grab my sister's wrist aggressively as soon as she walks out of the gate. "It's about time you came out. Come on, let's go."

Lindsay shakes my hand off her. "Let me say goodbye to Simon first."

I raise an eyebrow at her. When she says she wants to say goodbye, it's never a simple "bye" and a wave. No, it mostly involves cheesy couple stuff like 'I will call you later', 'No, I will call you later.' Blah, blah, blah. It's ridiculous. It makes me want to throw up every time I hear them say it. "Well, why don't you just say goodbye to him right now so we can get out of here?"

"Chill, Alex," Simon says, putting an arm around Lindsay's shoulders. "Stop hassling Lindsay to do the things you want her to do."

I give him a frown, biting the inside of my cheek. I did everything I could to restrain myself from wanting to punch his face in. If I wanted to, I could do it, but I couldn't do it here.

Lindsay smirks at me as Simon takes her hand and leads her away from me. Rather than using words to say goodbye, Simon wraps an arm around my sister's waist and pulls her closer to him before leaning in to kiss her. For a second, I watch them before I had to avert my gaze. No one else likely wanted to see them kiss, and I certainly didn't.

It's more than a minute, and I wasn't sure how much patience I had. Lindsay has pulled away from the kiss and holds onto Simon's hands, smiling as they talk. Yup, she is definitely testing my patience.

I inhale a deep breath before exhaling it, ready to lose my cool if my sister didn't hurry. "Can we go now, Lindsay?"

Lindsay only ignores me, her full attention on Simon. Without a word, I storm off to my car. Whether my sister was behind me, I didn't bother to wait for her to catch up to me. I'm sure she isn't in a hurry to get home at all.

I get in the car and drive past the entrance, where I see Simon and Lindsay had stopped talking. They were now wrapped in each other's arms. How long does it take to say goodbye to each other?

She is going to kill me for ditching her here, but I don't care. I wouldn't have left her behind if she hadn't come when I said to. Maybe next time she will say goodbye to her lousy boyfriend and follow me when I say so.

***

I've always enjoyed coming home to an empty house, a chance to have the place to myself with peace, even if it's only briefly. My mother won't be home until six o'clock, where she is the editor of the local newspaper. Lindsay may take a while to get home. She will get a ride with either Emilynn or Simon. God, I hope she doesn't get into the car with that jerk.

I walk upstairs to my room, dumping my bag on the floor. The first thing I do before I do anything else is get out of my ugly green school uniform, changing into a pair of jeans and a plain red t-shirt.

I take out my sketchbook and pencil from my bag, heading downstairs to the lounge room. I sit cross-legged on the couch just as I hear a car door closing from outside. It's probably Lindsay with whoever gave her a lift home. I open my book to the previous drawing I was working on earlier today and began shading some parts of the sketch.

The front door swings open. I look up for a brief second to see my sister walk through the door, and then turn back to my book.

I hear my sister's footsteps as she walks from the foyer to the lounge room. She says nothing, and I don't look up. I know she is standing at the doorframe of the lounge room. She is probably waiting for me to say something, but I don't know why I needed to say anything. There is nothing to say.

"I can't believe you left me behind at school," Lindsay says after a while. She moves to where she is standing at the doorframe and walks over to the couch. "You need to be patient and wait for me."

"If you want me to wait for you, then you shouldn't have made out with Simon," I tell her without looking up from my artwork.

"I wasn't making out with him," Lindsay tries to deny. "I was saying goodbye to him."

"You weren't saying goodbye to him, Lindsay. If you were, you would have said goodbye, kissed him quickly and then left. Not stand there and make out with him or take forever talking to him."

"Yeah, so? You could still have waited for a few seconds. I was only saying goodbye to him. I had to get Emilynn to drive me home because you left me behind."

"That's not my fault, is it?"

"Whatever, Alex," she replies, crossing her arms across the chest. "You still could have waited for me. Oh, and by the way, do you know what I heard about Nathan Bridges?"

No, and I don't really care.

"You asked him out, and he turned you down because he knows you aren't supposed to be dating two guys at the same time?" I answer instead.

I sneak a glance at my sister to see her reaction to my remark, which I know she won't like. She gives me a dirty look. I return my eyes to my drawing.

"No. That's not it. I heard he has a crush on you." She says it as if the words were poison.

I glance up at her, wondering if she was making it all up. Why would Nathan Bridges like me? I'm not girlfriend material, and I'm most definitely not interested in anyone.

I scoff. "Yeah, I'm sure he does."

I think back to recess today when I caught Nathan staring at me. Was he really staring at me or at someone else? No. There is no way that creep likes me. I don't believe he does. Lindsay is just screwing with my head only because she thinks I'm not normal for not having a boyfriend, which I don't want. I don't want anyone. She probably thinks she can hook me up with him. I will not let her do that.

Lindsay throws her arms in the air in frustration. "You know, I don't know why I even bother to talk to you. You're so useless."

"Well then, don't talk to me at all if you feel that way," I tell her. "I don't exactly want to talk to you either."

I go back to my drawing, feeling Lindsay's eyes on me.

"You know, I don't know what Nathan sees in you, but I definitely would never want to date you if I was him," she says. "What is wrong with your head? I just told you that a guy likes you. Can't you at least act normal and get excited? No guy has ever admitted he likes you. So why can't you at least appreciate it that someone likes you?" Under her breath I hear her say, "I know I would appreciate a guy noticing me."

I sigh with frustration. Does Lindsay really need to be telling me these things right now? I'm really not interested in knowing if Nathan likes me or not. Why should I appreciate him for noticing me? I have no desire to be in a relationship. I'm fine on my own. Why do I need a guy to make me feel special or happy?

"Lindsay, do me a favour and go tell someone who cares," I say without looking up.

"You're so pathetic, Alex."

I glance up from my artwork, narrowing my eyes at her. "Can you go away and leave me alone?"

Lindsay lets out a frustrated scream. Saying nothing else, she storms out of the lounge room, stomping her feet as she walks along the carpet. I go back to my drawing as I hear her continuing to stomp her feet up the stairs to her room. I smile to myself now that I'm alone again.

Chapter 5

It has always been a habit of mine to wake up early before anyone in the house. I can't seem to sleep in past 6:30am. Lindsay is the total opposite of me. Mum literally has to drag her out of bed in order for her to be ready on time for school.

Once dressed, I headed downstairs. Movement comes from my mother's room as I walk past it. She will come down as soon as she finishes getting ready.

I prepare a bowl of cereal and sit at the table. I enjoyed the five minutes I had to myself before my mother strolled into the kitchen. She greets me good morning, but I don't return the greeting. She turns on the coffee machine and pops two slices of bread into the toaster. Like we do almost every morning, we don't speak to each other, acting like we are strangers. I may be rude to my mother, but I just wanted to eat my food without having a conversation with anyone, especially first thing in the morning. It will lead to things I don't want to discuss, and the last thing anyone wants is an argument.

Lindsay doesn't join us in the kitchen until maybe about twenty minutes later. She greets Mum and ignores me as she walks over to the cabinet, grabbing a bowl. She fills it with cereal that is left out on the counter, along with the milk, before taking a seat across from me.

"What are you girls getting up to today?" Mum asks. "Anything exciting happening at school?" She takes a sip of her coffee.

Lindsay shrugs. "Nothing exciting ever happens at school. So yeah, I'm not getting up to too much today." She takes a spoonful of her cereal.

I make sure no one is looking my way and roll my eyes. I find it so unbelievable what Lindsay has said. She is forgetting that I can see right through her, knowing exactly what she is planning to do today. I can read her mind. Even if we aren't close sisters anymore, I can still read it. As twins, we shared a sixth sense of knowing what the other one is thinking. She is no doubt going to get another shot at getting Nathan to notice her.

"What about you, Alex?" Mum asks me. "Are you doing anything interesting today?" She takes a bite of her avocado toast.

I shrug without saying a word and continue eating my breakfast.

Mum waits for me to answer, and when she doesn't get a response from me, she continues speaking. "Girls, I'm going out with Dereck tonight."

At the mention of my mother's boyfriend's name, I glance up at her, narrowing my eyes. Dereck London. Mum has been seeing him for the past six months now. As soon as she told Lindsay and me she was dating again, I yelled. She and Dad may no longer be married, but I didn't want her to date anyone else. Why would she even think about dating another man? Dad left when Lindsay and I were twelve. I want to believe he will return. Mum may be ready to move on with another man, but I wasn't ready. Not for another man who thinks he can replace my father.

Lindsay, unlike me, is all for seeing our mum be with Dereck. She interacts with him as if he already were our father. He has the same laugh as Dad and a caring personality that I can see why Mum had fallen for him. Still, I didn't need a man like him walking into my life like he could replace my father.

Dereck will never replace my father.

"Jerk," I mumble, hoping Mum wouldn't hear me. She doesn't like it when I make rude remarks about Dereck, no matter how much I hated him.

But she hears me, shooting me a warning look about my behaviour towards him. "Alex, you know very well that I don't like you speaking that way about Dereck."

I shrug. "So?"

"So, I would like you to be more respectful towards him and give him a chance."

"I don't want to give him a chance."

I stand up and take my bowl over to the dishwasher, placing it inside.

"Alex, please," Mum begs. "I know you're mad at me for dating him, but I want you to at least get along with him. Dereck is trying his hardest for you girls to accept him. I know he isn't your father, and I'm not asking him to be. I just want you all to get along."

I close the dishwasher and look over at Mum. She is staring at me, waiting for me to answer. Lindsay is watching me also, chewing her food slowly, a smirk on her face, enjoying that I was in trouble with Mum.

"No," my tone firm. "I will never give him a chance. He can try his hardest for me to accept him, but I won't. I don't want to get along with him. You shouldn't be seeing him, anyway. Dad will be back. Don't you give a damn about how he will feel about you being with someone else?"

Mum gives me a disapproving look. "Alexander. Don't use that kind of language."

Lindsay scoffs. "You're seriously worried about Dad disapproving? It has been six years, Alex. Dad isn't coming home. He left us. Why would it matter to him if Mum sees someone else?"

I clench my jaw and then walk out of the kitchen before I get into a heated argument about my dad with my sister and mum. Not the first thing in the morning.

I head up to my room to gather my things for school. As I gather my things, I glance at the photograph of my dad and me beside my bedside table. In the picture I'm seven years old, sitting on his lap as we both pulled goofy faces at the camera. I stare at it, feeling this rip in my heart as I remember the day he had left. I didn't want to think about it, but it's something I can't just forget, not knowing the reason he never came home. Did he leave because of me?

I couldn't think of a single thing I had done that would have made him leave the morning of Lindsay's and my twelfth birthday. Out of all the days he could have walked out, why did he leave on our birthday? If he didn't leave because of me, was Lindsay the reason? Or was there another reason I don't know about? He couldn't have had a falling out with Mum. He loved her.

Didn't he?

Dad and I have always been close. We did almost everything together. I remember when he would sometimes come home from work and be so exhausted, but he still made time to sit down and draw with me. He was an artist himself, an architect. I learned to draw from him. He'd collect my drawings and place them in a folder for me to look back at someday and see how much I improved with my artwork. I still have the folder. It hides in the back of my wardrobe. I haven't looked through it in years, especially after he left.

And I don't plan to. Ever. The memories would be too painful.

But right now I did not have time to stop and think about the photo or memories of my dad. I have to get ready for school. I force myself to turn away, heading down the stairs. Mum comes rushing by when I reach the landing. She kisses my forehead, telling me to have a good day at school before rushing out the front door.

I stand in the doorframe, watching Mum get into her car that's parked behind mine in the driveway. Every time she leaves for work, a crazy thought always wanders into my head, wondering what happens if she doesn't return home. She wouldn't leave Lindsay and me like Dad did, would she?

I shake the thought out of my head. *She won't do that, Alex. Stop thinking like that.*

Once Mum is out of the driveway, I look around the house, wondering where my sister could be. No doubt she is even ready to leave for school.

"Lindsay, we are leaving in five minutes!" I call out to my sister. "If you aren't ready, I'm leaving without you!"

She comes running out of the kitchen and pushes past me up the stairs to her room. There is no way she will be ready in five minutes.

***

The drive to school was silent. It wasn't normal for us not to bicker whenever we are in the car together, but Lindsay's attention this morning was on her phone. I wasn't sure who she was texting. From the smile on her face, it could be Simon. Or maybe she was talking with Emilynn. It made me curious what she could talk to them about.

Once I park the car, Lindsay and I go our separate ways. I walk ahead of her. I see Simon with a bunch of his teammates from the school rugby team, standing at the bus bay where a coach is there to take them to another school for a game.

But surprisingly, Lindsay doesn't go to greet him. Instead, she makes her way over to Emilynn, who is standing by the entrance.

"Have you seen Nathan yet?" I hear Lindsay ask Emilynn the moment I walk past her friend.

I roll my eyes. What a slut. Is that all she ever thinks about? I turn to face them, throwing Lindsay a dirty look. Doesn't she know her boyfriend is near her? She sees my glance but ignores me.

I make way to the back of the library, sitting in my usual spot under the shelter to draw before roll call.

English was the first subject for the day again. The thought of Nathan sitting between us again after what Lindsay told me yesterday made me want to move somewhere else, but I couldn't when it's my required seat.

And with Simon away at football today, Lindsay will plan to flirt with him.

I focus on my work, copying what Mrs Callea was writing on the whiteboard about sentence structures into my notebook. From the corner of my eye, I see my sister trying to flirt with Nathan without being caught by Mrs Callea. I roll my eyes and shake my head, glancing over at Nathan. Whatever Lindsay was doing to get his attention, he wasn't taking an interest. I have to bite my lip to stop myself from laughing out loud. Lindsay whispers to him, saying how she doesn't understand what Mrs Callea was writing, and wanted Nathan to explain it to her. Instead of answering her, he keeps his focus on his own work.

When the bell rings for second period, Lindsay follows Nathan out of the room. That girl just doesn't know how to quit. I went in the opposite direction towards art so I didn't have to see her flirt with him.

Visual Arts is the only subject I enjoy. Sometimes I wish it was the only subject I could study for the HSC.

I pull out the canvas I have been working on in class for the past few days. On it, I have an outline of a rose with its petals falling to the ground in pencil. It's different to what I drew in my sketchbook, which I keep private. I normally drew whatever came to mind.

Grabbing some red and black paint, I pour it into a plastic plate. Before I paint, I experiment with mixing the colours together until I am happy with the shade of red I want. Sitting down in front of my canvas, I slowly paint the inside of the rose, careful not to go out of the outline.

My teacher, Mrs Hawkins, comes around to check how I'm doing. From the corner of my eye, I see her smile at my progress, her hazel eyes sparkling.

"Excellent work, Alex," she tells me.

"Thank you," I answer without looking up from my work.

"After class today, do you mind hanging back? There's something I would like to discuss with you."

I nod, wondering what my teacher wanted to talk about. "Sure."

Mrs Hawkins moves onto the next person, allowing me to keep going with my work.

Near me, I can hear Summer Anderson filling in the latest gossip with her friend Michelle Higgins as they work on their artwork. I tried not to listen in on their conversation as I concentrated on my work, but I couldn't help eavesdropping when they were talking loud enough for anyone to hear. The topic of her gossip is my sister. I never liked Summer. She is this snobby redhead who is worse than Lindsay with gossiping. It's like they needed to know what was going on in everyone's lives than worrying about their own.

"Did you hear what happened with Lindsay Jennings?" Summer says.

I peek over at the mention of my sister's name before turning back to my work.

Michelle shakes her head. "No. What?"

"I saw her flirting with Nathan Bridges in the corridor today on my way to class."

Michelle drops her paintbrush and looks at her friend. "No way! Isn't she dating Simon McGuire?"

Summer nods. "Yes, she is. You know what a slut Lindsay Jennings is."

I bite my lip to not say something nasty to Summer. Detention wasn't worth getting because she was dissing my sister. I knew Lindsay was a flirt, but I didn't appreciate what Summer was saying about her. If anyone is going to say something horrible about my sister, it will be me. Anyone else, you go through me if you want to say something about my sister.

"She is always flirting with guys," Summer goes on. "Anyway, she bumped into Nathan on purpose, dropping her books. He knows she likes him, and she asked him out yesterday. He rejected her. You will never guess who he admitted he liked."

My stomach twisted into knots. I had a feeling of what she was going to say, and I didn't want to hear it. It was bad enough that I heard it from my sister. I didn't need to hear it from someone else too.

Then again, hearing it from someone else other than my sister will confirm Lindsay wasn't lying. Nathan cannot like me.

"He likes her sister," Summer says.

At the mention of me, my stomach does a flip.

Michelle gasps. "No way! Alexander Jennings?"

I felt their eyes on me. I glance over my shoulder at them, only to find them not looking my way. They sat close to each other, giggling as they talked about how I would never get myself a boyfriend. I narrow my eyes at them. It's like they have forgotten that I'm in the same classroom as them, and I can hear everything they say. Maybe they wanted me to hear it, just to make myself feel bad. Why would I make myself feel bad? I'm perfectly happy the way I am being single.

I know I should say something to them, but I don't bother. There's no point telling them to shut up because they will keep saying nasty things about me or even someone else. A lot of popular girls in my grade gave me a hard time for not having a boyfriend. I don't see what the big deal is about having one. I don't want one. Guys aren't even worth being with, so why would I waste my time with one, only to get hurt later? They only play with your heart just to get what they want and then leave you when they are gone, stabbing your heart until you bleed out.

That's what Dad did to Mum. He left her. He left Lindsay and me, too. Everyone tells me he wasn't coming back. I refuse to believe them because in my heart; I know Dad will return... Someday. I don't know when, but I know he will come back for us.

Ignoring the girls, I went back to my painting. I don't have time to listen to them. Right now I just wanted to focus on my artwork.

***

Mrs Hawkins hands me a flyer for an art show once the other students have left for recess. It was later this year, in July. There was $1,000 for first prize in the competition.

I stare at the flyer in my hand, unsure how I should respond. What kind of artwork should I even display? The competition would want something spectacular, and I don't believe I would even have a chance out of all the competitors. I prefer to keep my drawings to myself instead of displaying them for all to see.

"I want you to enter this competition," she tells me. "Your artwork has really improved in the past year, and I think this will be an excellent way of showcasing your work."

"How do you know I will even be good enough for this?" I ask. Mrs Hawkins has only seen the work I have done for class, but she has never seen my private sketchbook.

My teacher smiles. "Because I know you're good enough, Alex. You're my best art student. Your art has a way of capturing emotions, and I believe this competition will be a great opportunity for you."

I shake my head, handing the flyer back to her. "Thanks, Mrs Hawkins, but I don't think so. This isn't for me."

Mrs Hawkins doesn't take the flyer. "Keep it on you. Just think about it, okay? And if you need the classroom to work on the project, just let me know. I will let you come in here either at lunch or an hour after school to work on it. I believe in you, Alex."

I force a smile. I thank her and then leave the classroom, shoving the flyer into my bag. There was no way I was entering this competition. No one would want to enjoy my drawings.

Chapter 6

The clock ticking in the lounge room is irritating. I can't even think because of it. It's past seven o'clock, and Mum still hasn't returned home. I don't know how long she will be out with Dereck. She's out to dinner with him a few nights a week, and if it's a Friday or Saturday, she stays out longer. During weekdays she tries not to stay out past eight o'clock. One time she came home at midnight. She does not know how much that stresses me when she is out so long. The last thing I wanted to think something had happened, or she decided she wasn't coming home like Dad did. But I remind myself that Mum won't be like him.

She will be home soon. Hopefully.

I sit beside the windowsill, peeking through the white curtains, watching for Mum's car, twisting the bracelets around my wrists. I have been sitting here since five o'clock, watching out for her and making sure she returns home safely. There's a frozen meal in the freezer that Mum had left for Lindsay and me, but I wasn't hungry. Even when my sister came downstairs to eat, I didn't move from the window. Each time a passing car comes, I get my hopes up it will be her, but then my heart crushes when it isn't.

There's an urge inside me to call her, finding out how much longer she is going to be, but I don't. She wouldn't like me calling her and pestering her about her date. Mum will only want me to call if it's an emergency.

A car soon pulls up alongside the kerb at the front of our house. A part of me is hoping it's Mum, but I know it isn't. It's dark out so I can't really see the car well from the window, and the streetlight wasn't bright enough. If it were Mum, she would have pulled into the driveway. I stare at the vehicle, watching as a dark figure emerges from it, making their way up the lawn to the front door. As the figure gets closer, the light from the veranda reveals who the person is. I narrow my eyes at him. What is he doing here?

Of course the answer was obvious to what that creep was doing at our house: Lindsay invited him. She always invited her boyfriend over when Mum wasn't home.

Simon couldn't see me through the window, but if he did, I'm pretty sure he would have turned and got back into his car from the death stare I am giving him.

He rings the doorbell, but I move from the windowsill to answer. There is no way in hell I was going to open the door for that idiot and allow him inside. Lindsay should come down soon. She can answer it since it's her guest. She will probably yell at me for not answering it. I don't need to let him in. I don't want him anywhere inside this house.

I hear my sister running down the stairs. I turn to her as she appears at the bottom. She wears her usual outfit–a blue denim mini-skirt and a pink camisole. Her feet are bare, so I guess she isn't planning on going out with Simon tonight. They are probably going to sit in her room and who knows what they will get up to. Not that I want to know, because I don't.

Simon rings the bell for the fifth time. I close my eyes, trying not to lose my cool over the doorbell. Counting to ten silently in my head, I try not to let the sound of the doorbell get to me. It doesn't help when the clock is ticking loudly either. All I want to do is rip the bell out. I don't know why someone even installed it.

"You know you could have let Simon in," Lindsay says when she spots me sitting on the windowsill.

"Whatever," I say. "He's your boyfriend."

Lindsay ignores my remark and walks over to the door, opening it. Simon greets her, stepping over the threshold.

"You look great, Lindsay," Simon says as Lindsay closes the door.

"Thanks, Simon. Shall we head upstairs?"

"Of course. But first, give me a kiss."

Simon rests a hand on her waist and pulls her close before planting a kiss on her. I watch them make out near the front door. When Simon slips a hand under her camisole, all I can imagine is pulling him away from her and throwing him out the front door.

"Hello?" I say, stopping their make-out session from going any further. "You aren't the only people in this house."

Simon and Lindsay turn to me, like they suddenly remember I was here.

"Well, no one said you have to watch," Lindsay snaps back at me. "Besides, it's none of your business what Simon and I do."

"Yeah?" I stand up, walking over to them. "It is my business, Lindsay. Especially if something happens to you or if you do something you would regret. And since Mum isn't here, I'm in charge. So, therefore, I say that Simon has to leave."

Lindsay rolls her eyes at me. "Oh, shut up, Alex. Just because you are three minutes older than me, it doesn't mean you're the boss of me."

Without another word to me, Lindsay walks up the stairs. She calls Simon to follow.

But he doesn't follow her up straight away. Instead, he walks closer to me. I step backward when he comes closer. The look in his eyes told me not to trust him.

"Do you have a problem with me, Alex?" he asks.

I cross my arms across my chest. "Do you really need me to answer that?"

"I don't understand why you're so angry every time I come over to spend time with my girlfriend. I treat her good. Don't you see that?"

I raise my eyebrow. Even if he does treat her good, he isn't exactly nice to me. "I just don't think you're worth my sister's time."

He scoffs. "Yeah? Well, I think you're a waste of air. No one likes you, so maybe you should just leave? Maybe disappear? Put yourself out of misery. It will be better than hating everyone."

Simon's words were like a knife had stabbed through my heart. It was bad enough Dad left me because I was probably not good enough for him, but Simon wanted me to actually disappear and put myself out of misery? All because I didn't think he was the guy my sister should hang around with?

My throat felt like it was closing up, making it impossible to respond, despite my efforts to think of something. Simon smirks before sticking his middle finger at me and runs up the stairs to follow my sister.

I stand there for a moment, wiping the tears that's forming in my eyes. *Don't let him get to you. He's a jerk, Alex.*

But still his words kept running through my head, and I can't help but think what if that's the reason Dad left? Did Dad not like me? Was I no longer good enough for him?

I sit back down on the windowsill, resting my head against the window. It was hard not to think of the things Simon had said to me that were now racing through my head. What if I were to disappear, walk out of everyone's life like Dad did? Would everyone be happy that I'm gone?

Tears start falling before I can stop them. I miss dad. I wish he were here right now. He would tell me I wasn't a waste of air. When I was upset about something, it wasn't Mum I went to. I went to Dad, and he always put a smile on my face. Since he is gone, I can't remember the last time I was happy. What happened the day before my twelfth birthday when he left? Did I do something wrong? Or maybe my mother and he got into a fight?

I wish I knew the answers to these questions.

Mum soon returns home at eight thirty. There's a sense of relief when I see her car, and I remind myself that there was nothing to worry about. She wasn't leaving like Dad. Now that she is home safely, I head up to my room. I don't wait for her to come in because she will ask me how I am. If she asks me, I might burst into tears. I don't want Mum to worry about me.

I rush up the stairs before she came in. As I passed my sister's room, I heard Simon and Lindsay laughing about something. I curl my hands into a fist, wondering if Lindsay would laugh if she knew her boyfriend had told me to disappear out of everyone's life? Did she even hear him say it? If she did, would she tell him off for saying those things? Or does she think I'm a waste of air too? It still made me wonder what she saw in that jerk.

Closing the door to my room, I hope to be alone for the rest of the night with no one disturbing me. Sitting down on my bed, I reach for my sketchbook from under my pillow. I open it to a clean page and begin sketching, trying my best to block out what Simon had said. The sudden sound of Lindsay broke my focus on drawing in the next-door bathroom. She is talking to someone, probably to Emilynn. I press my ear against the wall to hear what my sister is saying.

"Oh my gosh! Are you serious?" I hear my sister say. "You actually saw him in there?"

I roll my eyes and let out a sigh. It's definitely Emilynn on the other end of the phone. Whatever they are talking about, it must have something to do with Nathan. Who else would they be talking about? Definitely not Simon, who Lindsay seems to forget she is dating. I wonder if he was still here or if he had left already.

"I can't believe he is actually getting me flowers," Lindsay continues. "I knew he liked me. This is going to be the best Valentine's Day ever tomorrow."

I chuckle to myself when I heard her say that. Flowers? Really? Did she really think Nathan would buy her flowers? The guy doesn't even like her. And even if tomorrow is Valentine's Day, I doubt the creep will give her flowers. He is most likely getting it for someone else.

And I hope the person isn't me.

58

Chapter 7

I don't care if Mrs Callea requires me to sit in front of her desk to monitor me; I'm sitting at the back of the classroom this time. She was writing on the whiteboard when I entered the classroom and didn't notice me. I'm sure she will be relieved if I sit in the back. That way I didn't have to sit near my sister.

I keep my head down, focusing on my sketchbook as other students enter the room. They walk in, showing off the roses they got for Valentine's Day that were handed out this morning in roll call. Lindsay got a couple. One from Simon and I do not know who else had sent her a rose. No one sent me any, and I'm glad they didn't. I don't need a stupid rose from someone on a day where I'm sure no one really loves each other.

From the corner of my eye, I see someone approaching me. I snapped the book shut before they got a glimpse of what I was drawing. Once it's closed, someone places a single red rose down in front of me. I stare at it, not daring to look up to see who has placed it there. I have an idea who it might be, and I'm afraid to make eye contact with him. No one has ever given me a rose before. I'm surprised they are giving it to me in person. Why would they give me one? I don't deserve one. No one can ever like me. This has to be some kind of sick joke.

I can hear my classmates whispering, wondering how I'm going to react to this.

"Alright class, please settle down," Mrs Callea says. "Nathan, please take your seat so we can get started."

My teacher's voice snaps me out of my cone of silence. Nathan. Nathan Bridges. Of course it's him who placed the rose down on the table. He didn't even hand it to me. He just placed it down on my sketchbook, almost as if maybe he was afraid of what I would do if he had called my name and given it to me. Maybe Nathan thought placing it in front of me was easier than handing it to me. And why else would anyone place the rose there? After all, Emilynn had told my sister she'd seen him purchasing the rose. He had brought it for me. Out of all the girls in this school, why was he choosing to give me a rose?

I'm not a likeable person. I'm a waste of air, like Simon said last night. Why would Nathan want me?

He is still standing beside me, waiting for me to say something. What does he expect me to say? Thank you? Okay, so maybe I should say that, but my brain can't register the words.

I force myself to look at him, unsure what I should be feeling. Any girl would be over the moon from receiving a rose, but not me. A combination of confusion, shock, and anger takes over me, and I do not know which emotion to choose. I don't understand why he went through this trouble to give me a rose. Doesn't he realise I'm not interested? How do I know if he is really into me? What if he uses me for one thing only and dumps me later? Is that what he is planning to do?

I stand up from my desk, still dazed from this confusion. Nathan still hasn't moved. He stands there, waiting for me to say something. We ignore Mrs Callea, who is telling us to sit down. I can't bring myself to look at anyone but Nathan, even though I sense their gazes on us. I eye him, trying to read his mind about what he could see in me. He can't like me. Why would he want to like someone who doesn't want to love back, afraid to be hurt?

No, I can't like anyone. I don't care if Nathan has a crush on me. I will get hurt again if I even consider going out with him.

I turn from him and look down at the rose again. Mrs Callea is warning us that if we don't sit down we will get detention, but I drown out her voice. The rose torments me as it sits there on my book. I remember every year when Dad used to bring home roses for Mum, especially for Valentine's Day. Red roses are a symbol of love. Why is it a symbol for love? Love doesn't even exist. If it did, Dad wouldn't have left!

I let out a frustrated scream as I grab the rose, ripping the petals off the bud. I threw it at Nathan. He takes a slight step back, not expecting me to act like this. What? Did he honestly think I would accept it and then run into his arms and live happily ever after with him?

"Alex?" He suddenly realises his mistake, a hint of fear in his dark blue eyes, unsure of what I could do next.

I narrow my eyes at him, my blood racing to my head as the anger became too much for me. My head spins as the rest of my body shakes. I shove him hard in the chest. He tumbles backward into the person behind him, landing on the floor.

"Stay away from me, okay?!" I yell at him. "I don't like you! Do you hear me?"

Before Nathan answers me, Mrs Callea's voice scolds at me from across the room. "Alexander Jennings, I want you to go to the principal's office this moment. I am fed up with your behaviour this week. If you want to use violence, you can get out of my classroom."

I breathe heavily as I stand there staring at Nathan, not even sure why I had pushed him. This isn't something I normally do. I stay away from people, not use violence on them. It was like the anger shut my brain down when I thought about the way Dad had left Mum, causing me to not think about what I was doing when my hands lashed out at Nathan. It doesn't feel right for him to give me this rose. All of this feels like some kind of joke. Love is a joke. People use you for one thing. They use you to make you feel good, and then in an instant they can stab you in the heart, leaving you to bleed out when they walk away. I will not let him brainwash me into thinking he is a nice guy.

Saying nothing else, I gather up my things, not making any eye contact with my classmates. I especially don't look at my sister, knowing she will have a smirk on her face. I know what they are all thinking. That I, Alexander Jennings, have completely lost it, and that I should be consider being locked up in a psychiatric ward.

Or maybe they might think the same thing as Simon, and I should disappear. No, only Simon would suggest that. No one else would, would they?

Mrs Callea walks over to me and hands me a note to give to the principal.

I take the note and then hurry out of the classroom. Once I'm alone in the corridor, I take my time walking down to Mr Matthews' office. This isn't the first time a teacher has sent me to his office for some random act of violence or for back-chatting. Teachers keep sending me to see him every time they feel they can't deal with me. I don't know why they think shoving someone is violence. It's different if I had punched them. All I did was push Nathan, nothing else. And if I do back-chat, I'm just expressing my opinion. Teachers don't have to act so bitchy because of the things I say. They know I'm right. They just don't want to admit it.

Sometimes I'm surprised that my behaviour hasn't gotten me suspended or expelled. Mr Matthews doesn't tolerate violence in this school. I think he keeps me in school because he knows I'm an excellent student, but he also knows I have a lot of anger issues to sort out. He lets the school counsellor deal with me rather than helping me solve my issues himself. Some lousy principal he is. Mr Matthews used to give me detentions, but then he stopped, saying that I should seek help for my behaviour. He had even thought of suspending me once, and then decided not to. He informed my mother about sending me to see a counsellor, seeking professional help to sort out my anger issues. Yeah, right. Like a counsellor could help me. Mum agreed with his suggestions, not caring what I had to say about it all. I had no choice but to attend a counselling session at least twice a week. I know people think I'm insane, but that's no reason to send me to see a freaking counsellor.

I hated telling every single detail of my personal life to a therapist. Why should they even care what goes on in my life? They can't help me. They can't bring Mum and Dad back together.

"Hello, Alex," Mr Matthews greets me as I close the door to his office. "It's nice to see you again."

I scoff. "Yes, it's definitely nice to see you." I hand him the note Mrs Callea had written.

He takes it and reads it. In a calm voice, he says, "Why don't you take a seat, Alex?"

I listen to him without complaining and flop down on the chair in front of his desk. I place my bag on the floor and rest my sketchbook on my lap, not making any eye contact with him. Instead, I stare at his desk, which is a mess with all of his paperwork. Has he ever heard of keeping his desk clean?

He puts the piece of paper down and glances up at me. "In this note it says that you pushed Nathan Bridges."

I shrug, not really wanting to talk about it.

"Alex," his voice firm as he speaks, "this behaviour of yours needs to stop. I'm tired of teachers sending you in here because you have been back-chatting with them, or you're using some kind of violence against other students."

I raise an eyebrow at him. "Violence? Back-chatting? Really? I only give them my opinion about something, and they call that back-chat? And since when is shoving a person violence?"

Mr Matthews inhales a breath before letting it out, and then leans forward on his desk, folding his arms. "Alex, I can understand what must be going on through your mind, but–"

"You don't know what's going through my mind."

"Okay, maybe I don't exactly understand, but you need to realise that whatever issues you have, keep them to yourself and don't let them out on other people."

I lean back on the chair and cross my arms across my chest.

"How is the counselling going with Miss Giovanni?" he wants to know.

I frown. "Why do you want to know?"

"Well, you have been seeing her since I suggested her to your mother. It doesn't seem like you have sorted your issues out yet. You seem to hold on to them and throw them in other people's faces."

I look down at my fingers and clean some of the dirt from under my fingernails, just to avoid answering the principal. He doesn't need to know my business. And what right does he have to speak to me like that? Whatever the school counsellor and I talk about, he doesn't need to know.

When he saw I wouldn't answer him, Mr Matthews let me go. I get up, glad I didn't have to be sitting in his office anymore, and hurried out the door. As I put my hand on the knob, he tells me to go to the counsellor's office before I head back to class. I roll my eyes and let out a frustrated sigh. Mr Matthews does this every time he doesn't know how to handle me. He sends me to Miss Giovanni, hoping she knows what to say to me in the hope I would change my ways.

I didn't want to see Miss Giovanni. Not today. I wasn't in the mood to talk to her at the moment.

The counsellor's office is just across from the principal's office. I pray silently to myself she wouldn't be in today, but the chances are slim. She barely takes a day off from work. She is always there. Besides, even if I decide to skip my session with her, Miss Giovanni will know I did. Mr Matthews has already gotten on his phone to notify her to let her know I was coming before I even walked out of his office.

Even though I disliked the counsellors Mum had tried to get me to see outside of school, which thankfully I don't see anymore, Miss Giovanni is the only one I didn't mind seeing. The others, I don't feel like they can help me out with my problems. They don't seem like they wanted to listen. Miss Giovanni really listens to you, no matter what you're going through. She has this soft, gently voice that always makes you feel welcome and comfortable. Her long black hair is always hanging loose around her shoulders. I have never seen it pulled back once. I like her eyes. They're this really nice deep brown. She also has a couple of freckles on her nose, and looks to be around her mid-twenties.

I step over the threshold of Mr Matthews' office, closing the door behind me. Resting my back on the door, I closed my eyes for a second, sighing. I hate being forced to see the counsellor to talk about my problems, even if Miss Giovanni is nice. Sometimes I prefer to keep it all to myself.

I stare at the door to Miss Giovanni's office. It's open just a crack. I hesitated whether I should make a run. I ran away once when she asked to see me. Mr Matthews came looking for me, finding me in the library during lunch. He dragged me to her office.

Taking a deep breath, I walk over to the door and stand there, knocking softly. I hear movement coming from inside her office. A few seconds later, the door opens and Miss Giovanni stands there in the doorway.

She smiles when she sees me. "Hello, Alex. Mr Matthews just called me to let me know you were coming to see me. Come on in and take a seat."

She moves aside so I could walk in and closes the door behind me. I take a seat in front of her desk. She walks around to her desk, telling me to wait for a second as she clears away some papers and puts them aside.

I glance around the room in the meantime as I wait for her. The office is small. Behind her, she has university degrees in frames. She has a bulletin board to one side of the frames with brochures for personal problems like domestic violence, bullying, mental health, and something with disabilities. Near the window of her office is a bookshelf full of books, papers and folders. Behind me are three filing cabinets.

She grabs a manila folder sitting beside the stack of papers she had just put aside. I see my name written on the folder, and she opens it and takes a pad of lined paper in front of her. Sometimes I'm curious about what notes she writes about me each session.

Miss Giovanni looks up at me and smiles. "It's good to see you again, Alex. How has your morning been?"

I raise my eyebrows at her. Is she seriously asking me that? "Do I really have to explain?"

She shrugs. "Well, you don't have to if you don't want to. We can talk about something else if you prefer. Do you want to tell me what's bothering you?"

I sigh with frustration, not exactly wanting to tell her anything. But I do. I tell her about the rose Nathan gave me, and how I had thrown it in his face. It makes me wonder why he handed it to me in person, and not when the school council went around handing out roses that morning. Why would he want to give it to me in person, and not do it the way the rest of the school was hanging out their Valentine's roses?

"Why do you feel you had to act the way you did, Alex? You could have politely turned him down and said you aren't interested in going out with him."

"Well, how else am I going to get him to see that I have no interest in wanting to go out with him? I catch the guy watching me sometimes, and it makes me uncomfortable."

"I'm sure there are other nicer ways you could have told him you aren't interested instead of shoving him, Alex."

"Whatever," I mumble softly. I'm sure my actions today have shown Nathan that I want nothing to do with him.

I glance down at my hands, noticing the dirt has returned underneath my fingernails again after I cleaned it in Mr Matthews' office.

Miss Giovanni notices how I don't want to talk anymore, nor do I want to be here, but she tries to keep me talking anyway. "Have you mentioned to Nathan that his staring makes you uncomfortable?"

"No," I say without looking up at her. "But I'm sure after today he won't be."

She nods slowly. "Is there anything you would like to mention about Nathan, or how you're feeling?"

"No."

"Maybe you want to explain to me what made you get upset over the rose?"

"No."

"We can talk about something else."

I groan. Do we really need to talk?

"Or we don't have to talk at all. It's your choice. We can sit in silence."

Or you could just let me go? I wanted to say.

I mean, why let me stay in this office when Miss Giovanni knows I don't want to be here?

"How is your drawing going?" Miss Giovanni asks.

"It's good," I answer.

"Can I see what you have drawn lately?"

At first I don't move. I stare down at the sketchbook in my lap for a few minutes before deciding to hand it over. I watch as she flips through it to see what I have drawn. When I first started seeing her, Miss Giovanni said I didn't have to show her my drawings I drew of my dad, but she insists I show her. That way she can help me. There was something about her that made me trust her with my book. Maybe because whatever is said in this room stays between us, and that's why I trust her not to tell anyone about my drawings.

But I honestly don't know how she can ever help me through the broken heart I had when Dad walked out on my twelfth birthday.

"You're still drawing pictures of your father?" she asks me without looking up from my book.

"It's the only way I can express what I think of my dad," I answer.

Ever since Dad had walked out on my family almost six years ago, instead of telling people how I felt about him leaving, I drew pictures of him, of memories I have had of him from over the years. I don't like to talk about him much, even with Miss Giovanni. She has tried so many times to get me to talk about him with her, but she respects my wishes when I don't want to say anything. No one understands what my dad means to me. No one understands how I feel. Not even my sister or Mum knows, though they had gone through the same thing as me.

People say they understand how I feel, but truthfully they don't.

"Each time I look at these drawings, they get even better," Miss Giovanni says as she looks up at me and smiles. "Have you thought about drawing something else besides your father?"

"I don't exactly care about anything else. I don't even like it when Mrs Hawkins encourages us to express ourselves in different ways in Visual Arts, because it means going out of my comfort zone where I only feel comfortable with drawings of my dad. It's how I express myself, reflecting on memories of him. Mrs Hawkins even approached me yesterday, wanting me to join an art competition."

Miss Giovanni smiles. "That's great, Alex. Are you going to enter?"

I shake my head. "No. I don't want to. Not if I can't do a drawing of my dad. Mrs Hawkins wouldn't want that, and I don't want anyone to see it."

"I think the competition will be good for you, Alex. And there's nothing wrong if you express yourself differently. And I'm sure you could still enter a piece of artwork that could express yourself with your father. That's the beauty of art, Alex. Expressing yourself in different ways. Wouldn't it be better than drawing the same thing repeatedly?"

I shrug. Maybe it would be, but drawing pictures of my dad makes me happy. Like he is still part of my life.

Miss Giovanni closes the sketchbook. "Think about it, Alex. I'm sure you will do well in the art competition." She smiles, handing the book back to me.

I take it, placing it on my lap.

"Now, let's go back to what happened with Nathan," she continued. "Alex, why do you feel you need to turn him down the way you did?"

I shrug, biting down on my lip. "I don't want to be in a relationship. Guys aren't worth it."

"Do you think you could have approached this differently rather than using violence? You could have calmly told him you aren't interested."

I roll my eyes, sighing. Why is everyone making this a big deal when I pushed Nathan? "I wasn't being violent. I only pushed him."

"Alex, shoving someone still classifies as being violent. We don't have to do it today, but maybe at the next session we could work on your anger. So the next time Nathan or someone else asks you out, you could calmly say, 'Thank you, but I'm not interested' in a nicer way rather than lashing out at them."

"Whatever."

Miss Giovanni tries to make another attempt to get me to talk, but when I don't, she doesn't push me. She dismisses the session and allows me to head back to class.

Leaving her office, I closed the door behind me. I lean up against it, clutching my sketchbook to my chest. Tears fill my eyes, wishing Miss Giovanni had never brought up the topic of my father. Every session she tries to get me to talk about him, and I know it's something I could have spoken to her today, but I don't like to talk about him with anyone. I miss him so damn much it hurts. Though I miss him, I'm angry at him for leaving. It has been six years, and he caused so much damage to our family. Not talking about him is easier than having to express feelings. Lindsay never talks about him, or even seems to care that he is no longer a part of our lives. I don't want it being just Mum, Lindsay and me. I want Dad to be here where he belongs.

And then there's Dereck walking into our lives. Every time he comes over, there's an ache in my heart. Like he's some stranger trying to replace my father. Mum tells me to give him a chance, but I don't know how I do that. How do I give Dereck a chance when all I can think about is Dad? I mean, I can see why Mum has fallen for Dereck: He is kind and caring–the same personality as dad and it only breaks my heart more knowing that the one person I care about doesn't even care about me. Seeing Dereck with Mum brought back memories of how Dad was with her, and I wondered how things would be if he hadn't walked out?

I think about what it would be like if my dad came back home. How will I react if I saw him again? Would I yell at him? Most likely. Welcome him with open arms? Maybe not. I constantly replay the day when Lindsay and I woke up on our twelfth birthday to find Mum in the kitchen crying, and Dad wasn't around. I waited, wanting him to come home from wherever he'd disappeared to, wanting to spend my birthday with my family. But he never returned home. Every time Lindsay and I asked Mum when he was coming home, she would burst into tears.

I miss my dad. I want him to come home. Why is that too much to ask?

But it was no use wishing it. It was clear I didn't matter to my father. He was never returning home.

A part of me wanted to go back into Miss Giovanni's office and open up to her about my father. If not about Dad, I could talk to her about what Simon had said to me last night. But I don't. I step away from the front door and head back to class. First period was almost over, so I fake my time walking to English, hoping the bell would ring before I even had the chance to step foot in the classroom. I couldn't go back in there right now, and I'm sure Mrs Callea wouldn't be pleased if I returned.

And Nathan, I didn't want to face him right now.

Chapter 8

I keep my head down when I return to class to avoid eye contact with anyone. Especially with Nathan. What could he be thinking when he sees me? I can feel my classmates' eyes on me. Before I can sit down in my seat, the bell for second period rings. Mrs Callea calls me over to her before I had the chance to escape. Lindsay bumps into me on purpose on her way out, making me drop my sketchbook. She whispers "bitch" loud enough for me to hear, but not too loud for our teacher to hear. I wanted to say something in return, but I'm already in trouble and don't want to be in anymore. I pick up my book and then join my teacher at the front, preparing myself to be lectured by her.

"What was that, Alex?" she scolds, shaking her head. "I don't know what you were thinking, but I will not tolerate that kind of behaviour in my class."

"What behaviour? Shoving someone to get away from me?"

She gives me a warning look not to back-chat with her.

I sigh. "Look, I'm sorry, Mrs Callea. Nathan made me so mad. I pushed him to get the message that I wanted him to stay away from me."

Mrs Callea frowns. "I don't care if he made you mad. That's still no excuse for what you did, Alex. You could have injured him or someone else. I'm also not the one you should apologise to. The person to whom you should apologise to is Nathan."

I feel sick to my stomach. I can't apologise to him. Why should I be the one to apologise? If he hadn't approached me in the first place, maybe I wouldn't have acted the way I did.

When I say nothing else, Mrs Callea continues. "Please do not act the way you did in my class again. Not just with Nathan or with your sister, but with anyone in this class. I do not need you interrupting my class every time because you dislike something someone has done or what they say." She picks up some papers from her desk, shuffling them into a neat pile. "Now, here is the work I want you to complete. I know you and your sister have some rivalries with each other, but I want you to get the notes off her. If she refuses, then tell her I said she has to give you the notes she has written."

I restrain to roll my eyes in front of my teacher. Did she really expect me to ask Lindsay to copy her work? She doesn't even pay attention in class, so I know it was very unlikely that she had taken any notes at all.

Mrs Callea dismisses me, and I head out to my next classroom. I get a few metres down the corridor when someone walks alongside me. I don't have to look to see who it is. Lindsay was most likely standing nearby, eavesdropping on Mrs Callea and me. I don't stop for her, so she walks in front of me to get my attention, walking backwards. Ignoring her, I move around her, but she is too quick for me, blocking me from going anywhere.

"Get out of my way, Lindsay," I snap at her.

"I can't believe what you did to Nathan," Lindsay says, completely ignoring me. "What were you thinking?"

I sigh, rolling my eyes. "Leave me alone, Lindsay. I'm not in the mood to explain anything. Anyway, don't you have somewhere you need to be instead of bugging me? Like getting to second period?"

"You're never in the mood to talk. Nathan didn't deserve what you did. He was just being nice to you, hoping you would accept the rose." She stops talking when she notices the tears in my eyes. "Wait. Are you crying?"

I wipe my eyes. "No."

"Yes, you are."

"Why would you care if I am?"

"Mr Matthews sent you to see Miss Giovanni, didn't he? You always cry after seeing her. What do you talk to her about that makes you cry all the time?"

Did she really wanted to know? "Do me a favour and leave me alone, Lindsay."

I push past her and quickly take off down the corridor before my sister has the chance to catch up with me again. I needed to get to German before I'm late.

I wipe my eyes as more tears fall. I don't want anyone to see the tears or they would stop to ask me questions I don't want to answer.

"*Guten Tag*, Alex," Mr Brown greets me warmly at the classroom door.

Ignoring his greeting, I walk right past him and took my usual seat in the back row beside the window. I open up my sketchbook to draw, but close it when I see Mr Brown approaching me from the corner of my eye.

He kneels down in front of my desk, a concern look in his eyes. "Is everything okay, Alex?"

One by one my classmates enter the classroom, and I can feel their eyes on me, wanting to know what is happening. An urge built up inside me, wanting to scream at the top of my lungs, wanting everyone to leave me alone, but I bit my lip so I couldn't blurt anything out. The last thing I wanted was to be sent down to the principal's office again. Mr Matthews wouldn't be pleased to see me a second time, especially in a short amount of time. I'm sure he will issue me a detention if I'm sent to him again.

"I'm here if you ever want to talk," Mr Brown goes on when I don't respond.

"I'm fine, okay?"

"Alex–"

"For crying out loud, I'm fine!" I almost screamed it out. "If I really want to talk, I will say so. It's none of your damn business why I'm crying, so can you just leave me alone?"

Mr Brown stands, stunned by my words. He takes a step back and, without saying another word to me, walks to the front of the classroom to start the lesson.

Wiping my eyes, I open my sketchbook and pull out a pencil. Ignoring my teacher, I began drawing.

I feel someone's eyes on me. I turn to my right and see Nathan staring at me from across the room. As soon as I lock eyes with him, he turns and pretends to be listening to whatever Mr Brown is talking about. His friend, Eric, is sitting beside him. He whispers something to Nathan. I turn away from him and continue with my work.

Chapter 9

How to get my sister to hurry after school: She has a date tonight with Simon, and that was the only reason she didn't keep me waiting this afternoon. It was alright for her to keep me waiting at other times when I wanted to leave and not wait around for her, but today it was all about her and her date.

With my sister upstairs, I sit in the lounge room, resting my back up against the couch. I flip through the photo album in my lap, trying to pick out a photo to sketch.

I have flipped through this album so many times, getting lost in nostalgia. Filled with amazing memories of my dad that seemed so long ago now. I pull out a photo, one I remembered the day clearly, and smile. The photograph was of me at age five, sitting on my dad's shoulders, taken at the beach one summer day. He was shirtless while I had a pink flower swimsuit with a matching hat. White sunscreen was on my nose. I was laughing while Dad made a face into the camera. Lindsay was sick that day, where she had gotten heatstroke. I remember the day when Dad would always give both Lindsay and me a ride on his shoulders. I was the one who got to ride on him the most, more than Lindsay because she had a fear of heights and hated the idea of being so high on his shoulders.

I wish I could go back to those days when we were one big happy family. What made our family drift away? What made Dad leave?

I put away the photo album under the coffee table. I sit back on the couch and open up to a clean page of my sketchbook. Carefully copying the photograph, I sketch out Dad's goofy face.

For a moment, I sit there and just stare at the photograph. Though the photo was taken thirteen years ago, long before Dad left us, I wondered if there were any signs that perhaps Dad wasn't happy with us. I tried to think of a time when I thought maybe he wasn't happy, but there were no signs. He was always laughing happily and playing with my sister and me. After dinner he would sit with me to draw, teaching me all forms of art from painting and drawing to playing with clay. How did we go from being a happy family to a broken one?

I'm lost in my thoughts as I draw, spending half an hour on it before Lindsay enters the lounge room. I glance up at her, taking in the outfit she was wearing. She wore a black dress that barely covered her butt. Ignoring her, I went back to my drawing. How on earth can Lindsay wear something like that?

"What do you think of this outfit?" Lindsay asks, swirling around to give me a full view of it. "Do you think Simon will like it?"

I didn't answer her straight away, keeping my eyes on my drawing. Without looking at her, I say, "You're kidding, right? You're seriously going to wear that? It barely covers your butt. It's terrible. And of course Simon is going to like it. Any shorter and you might as well not be wearing it."

Lindsay frowns. "Can't you say something nice for once?"

I glance up at her. "What do you want me to say? That your outfit looks great?"

"Of course I would like you to say that."

"Well, I can't say it. But if you don't want to hear my opinion, then do whatever you want."

My sister narrows her eyes at me. "You know, Alex, it really wouldn't kill you to say something nice for once. You hating everything is getting old. I got this dress on sale, and I love it, no matter what you say."

"Yeah, whatever. Any dress would look nicer if it didn't make you look like a slut. Mum would not approve."

"Well, Mum isn't here. Seriously, Alex." She throws her arms in the air. "Why can't you just be nice for once? It's not that hard to do so. At least tell me if I look nice! Act the way a sister should and not like someone who is heartless. All I want to do is look my best for my date with Simon.

It's our one-year anniversary tonight. He has something special plan for me."

I arch my eyebrows. "Something special? Linds, the way you dress, I don't think you will make it out of this house. Anyway, why are you telling me this? I couldn't care less about your date with that jerk."

"I'm telling you this because you are my sister, Alex! I want you to be happy for me and tell me how great I look for my date. And Simon is not a jerk."

I scoff. "You want me to tell you how slutty you look for your date with Simon, who only wants to get in your pants?"

Lindsay chews the inside of her cheek as she frowns at me. She looks like she wants to say something nasty to me, but she decides against it. Instead, she flips her middle finger at me. I return the gesture.

"You're so unbelievable," she says before storming away. "All I want is to ask you to answer my question, but you always have to provide a bitchy comment. And who cares if Simon wants to get into my pants? We have had sex so many times. Maybe what you need is to get laid and then you wouldn't be so up yourself."

"Yeah, well, maybe you should break up with Simon. Do you know what he said to me the other night? He told me I'm a waste of air and I should disappear."

Lindsay turns back to me, frowning. "Simon did not say that. He would never say that."

"He did, Lindsay. How can you date someone like him?"

Lindsay scoffs. "Wow. Is this your way of telling me how much you hate my boyfriend?" She shakes her head. "I'm not breaking up with him, Alex."

"Really? Then why do you want to go out with Nathan so bad if you don't want to break up with Simon?"

"Even if I do, it doesn't mean I want to break up with Simon."

Without another word, Lindsay leaves the lounge room and runs up the stairs before I had the chance to respond, slamming her bedroom door behind her.

I sit there in silence, my heart crumbling in my chest. It's so quiet in here that the clock ticks loudly. How could Lindsay not believe me? Did she not hear him say it when she stood at the top of the stairs? Surely she would believe me and understand how I truly felt about her boyfriend. But unfortunately, she doesn't believe me. Would Miss Giovanni have believed me if I had told her about it today?

If Dad were here, he would believe me. He would have banned Simon from coming to this house. And he will definitely forbid Lindsay from dating him.

"You're not a waste of air," I whisper to myself.

I went back to my drawing, telling myself not to worry about the things Simon had said, even if they bothered me. I won't let that jerk think he can tear me down like he did. The sound of the pencil scribbling on the paper calms me.

Then, out of nowhere, the landline rings. I groan. What now? Can't everyone let me sketch in peace? I place my sketchbook on the table and hurry to the doorframe of the kitchen and lounge room, where the cordless phone is on a table. I was the only one who used the landline, as both my sister and Mum had their own phones. Mum wants to disconnect it, but because I refuse to own a phone, Mum kept it for me.

I let out a frustrated sigh before answering. "Hello?"

"Hi, I was just wondering if I could speak to Alex?" a guy's voice asks.

Okay, who on earth is calling me? No one ever calls me.

"You're talking to her. Who is this?"

"Hi, Alex. It's me, Nathan."

I almost drop the phone when he said his name. Nathan Bridges? Is he going to stalk me by phone now? How on earth did he get my number? Why is he calling me? Doesn't he have anything else to do? I thought I made it clear to him that I do not want to go out with him when I told him off today?

"Nathan? As in Nathan who handed me a rose in English today?" I ask. I knew it was Nathan Bridges, as he was the only Nathan in our grade, but I wanted to believe it was someone else, or someone with the wrong number.

"Yes, that's me."

I roll my eyes and sigh. What is it about today where everyone just seems to think it was okay to bother me? Can't people see I want to be left alone?

"What do you want now, Nathan? Was shoving you out of the way not clear enough that I'm not interested?"

"I just want to talk to you, Alex."

"Well, I don't want to talk to you, okay? I don't like you. Get that into your head. I. Do. Not. Like. You."

I hung up the phone without a goodbye. Before I could walk away, the phone rang again. I groan in frustration. That better not be Nathan. If it is, I'm going to scream.

I answer the phone on the second ring. "What now?"

"Hi." I recognise his voice straight away, as if he was afraid to even speak. "It's me again."

I roll my eyes. This guy really doesn't know how to quit. Why can't he get it through his thick skull that I'm not interested?

"How on earth did you get this number?" I wanted to know.

Nathan doesn't answer straight away. "I asked Lindsay for it."

Lindsay gave it to him. Of course that bitch did.

I slam the phone down. What did Lindsay think would happen if she got Nathan to call the landline? Hoping to piss me off? Or maybe she hoped to be the one to talk to him if she had answered? If she liked him so much, why didn't she give him her number instead of the landline?

The phone remains silent for a few minutes until I'm about to step away. It rings for the third time! For crying out loud, *I'm going to kill Lindsay!* Can't this idiot take a hint that I don't like him, nor do I want to talk to him? This time I threaten to him if he calls me again. I slam the cordless phone down hard on the phone holder, waiting for a few minutes before I move away in case that idiot calls again. I smile once I realise my threat worked. Good. He can annoy someone other than me.

I settle back down on the couch and resume my drawing. Hopefully, this time there won't be any more interruptions. Is it too much to ask that I want to be left alone?

It has only been two minutes when the front door opens and there goes my peace. Mum walks in followed by Dereck. I narrow my eyes at him. Does he seriously have to walk into this house like he lives here?

Mum walks into the lounge room, smiling. "Hi, Alex. How was your day?"

I keep my focus on Dereck instead of answering my Mum. "What are you doing here?"

Dereck looks at me like he is unsure if he should flee. I think he should flee and get out of our lives. "Your mother invited me to dinner."

I glance at my mother, frowning. She knows I don't like Dereck being here, so why does she do it?

Mum returns a look that tells me to be nice. "Dinner will be ready in about an hour, sweetie. Where's Lindsay? Is she in her room?"

"Yeah, and she is planning to go out with Simon tonight," I answer.

Mum smiles. "Okay, well I guess it will be the three of us tonight. Make sure you do your homework. I will be in the kitchen."

Mum leaves the room. Dereck stands next to the couch, eyeing my sketchbook on my lap. He smiles at me, as if he were hoping I would be friendly in return. I expected him to step away from the death stare I give him, but he doesn't move.

When I look at Dereck, I can't figure out why Mum likes him. Sure, he's handsome, with broad shoulders and was tall, possibly the same height as Dad. His hair is short, brown and greying at the roots. His brown eyes are soft, reminding me of Dad's. Every time I see him, I just want to scream.

"Alex, I'm so glad you're here," he says. "I was telling your mother that I brought tickets to an art exhibition next month. I was thinking about you, and thought you might like to come with me."

I stare at him. Was he serious? Dad used to take me to art exhibitions, where he thought it would inspire my art. What is Dereck expecting me to say? Yes? Why was he trying so hard for me to like him? I was not going anywhere with him where he thought he could replace my dad. He was *nothing* like my dad.

I stand up, gathering my belongings. "No."

"Are you sure?" Dereck asks. "This will be a great opportunity for you."

"Maybe it is. But I also don't need you to replace my dad."

Without another word, I leave the room and head up to my room.

***

I hear the doorbell ring from my room. Simon is here. I put down my English book and step over to the window that faces the street. Glancing out, I see my sister walking down the front lawn with Simon, hand in hand. The thought of what the two of them will get up to tonight disgusted me. I watch them until they get into Simon's car, disappearing down the street. How can Mum let her go out with that jerk?

I head downstairs to take a break from my homework. Being downstairs was the last thing I wanted with Dereck down there. Dinner should be soon. I walk into the kitchen to see Dereck setting the table. His back is to me. I narrow my eyes at him. I really hate how he parades around the house like he lives here. Or when he tries to act like a father to Lindsay and me.

He will never be my father.

"Oh good, Alex, you're here," Mum says from where she was standing at the stove. "I was just about to come get you."

I watch her as she grabs the pot and moves over to the counter, plating the spaghetti onto three plates. Ignoring Mum, I sit down at the table. Dereck pours a glass of water and then places it down in front of me. I frown. Did he really think water is what I would like to drink? He couldn't have asked me instead of assuming what I wanted?

I grab the glass and stroll over to the sink. I tip it down the drain.

"Sorry, Alex," Dereck apologises. "I didn't know what drink you wanted. I thought you might like water. Your sister always has water."

I place the glass on the counter and turn to him. "I'm not my sister. You could have asked me what I wanted."

"I'm sorry."

I walk over to the fridge and grab a bottle of Coke. Mum comes over to me, grabbing my arm aggressively before I had the chance to close the fridge door, and made sure I look at her.

"I want you to be nice to Dereck, Alex," she scolds. "I know you dislike him, but I want you to be nice. You hear me? I want you to like him. I know he isn't your father, but the least you can do is try to show some respect. Now, apologise to Dereck."

I roll my eyes and sigh.

She points her finger at me, frowning. "Don't you dare roll your eyes at me when I tell you to do something."

I turn to Dereck, who is standing there watching us. "I'm sorry."

He gives me a small smile. "It's fine."

I pour myself a glass and sit down at the table. Dereck sits across from me where Lindsay usually sits. Mum sets our plates on the table before taking her seat between us.

We eat in silence. I keep my eyes focused on my food so I didn't have to look at Dereck. I ate quickly so I could escape the silence. Mum has her eyes on her food, stirring her fork around her food, lost in thought. Something was on her mind, or she was probably trying to figure out what to say without me getting all bitchy about it.

I dump my cutlery into the dishwasher once I'm done and leave the room. Mum doesn't speak until she thinks I'm completely out of earshot. She doesn't realise that I'm standing beside the doorframe, resting my back up against the wall so I could hear what she has to say.

"I'm really sorry about Alex," she says.

"Jean, it's okay," Dereck answers. "I will not let her upset me."

"No. It's not okay, Dereck. I want Alex to show some respect for you, whether you're her father."

"Alex is a teenager. She's going through a lot, especially with her father walking out. I told her about the art exhibition, and she said no because she thinks I'm replacing her father."

"See, Dereck. I can't keep letting her use it as an excuse that you're replacing her father. It's no reason for her to treat you like crap. I figured she would be over it by now like Lindsay is. Yes, I totally understand why Alex is angry about what happened, but I wish she didn't drag everyone into it. I want her to be happy and accept you for who you are, and not my ex-husband."

I peek around the corner of the door. Dereck rests his hands on my shoulders. Seeing him do it reminded me of when Dad used to do the same thing to Mum when he showed sympathy whenever she was upset. I frown at him. Can he stop acting like my dad?

"Give her time, Jean," Dereck tells her.

Not wanting to hear any more of their conversation, I turn and head upstairs.

Chapter 10

"I didn't hear you come in last night, Lindsay," Mum says when we are sitting at the table the next morning. "Did you and Simon have a good night?"

Lindsay's face lights up, and she fills her in about her date. I sit there, tuning out my sister's voice and concentrating on my breakfast. Why should I hear about what she got up to with her lousy, reckless boyfriend? I don't want to know what the two of them got up to. It's bad enough when I witness them making out sometimes.

Mum turns to me once my sister finished speaking, asking how the rest of my night went when I left Mum and Dereck after dinner. I shrug with nothing to say, continuing to eat my cereal without looking up. What can I say about the rest of my night? I stayed in my room to complete my English homework and drew in my sketchbook, only so I could avoid Dereck. He didn't leave our place until midnight.

"Oh, Alex, did Nathan call at all yesterday?" Lindsay wants to know.

I look up from my bowl when she mentioned his name. I narrow my eyes at the thought of the many times he had called. He never called back again after I had threatened him.

"He called all right," I tell her. "He called at least three times while you were upstairs getting ready for Simon." I scoop up some cereal with my spoon. "Thank you for giving him our number. Now the jerk is going to be calling here all the time."

Lindsay frowns. "Nathan is not a jerk."

I stuff the spoonful of cereal into my mouth. "Yes, he is."

"Alexander, don't speak with your mouth full," Mum scolds. She looks between my sister and me. "So, who is Nathan?"

I roll my eyes. Do we really need to talk about Nathan Bridges this morning? "He is the most annoying jerk in the entire world."

"Actually, Nathan Bridges is a very sweet guy," Lindsay explains to Mum, which I didn't want her to know about. She will want to know all the details. There was nothing to talk about Nathan and me, because there is no us and never will be. "He is in our English class. I think he also takes German with Alex. Oh, and he has a crush on her as well."

I drop my spoon, letting it clatter loudly against the bowl, and then lean back on my chair. She just had to say that, didn't she?

Mum looks over at me, surprise. She always hears about my sister's crushes, and this is the first time she is hearing about someone liking me. She smiles. "Oh, does he? What do you think of him, Alex? Has he asked–"

"I don't like him," I answer quickly.

Making sure Mum wasn't looking, Lindsay throws me a dirty look. I don't know why. Perhaps it's because she was the one crushing on Nathan, and she didn't like the things I was saying about him. She can like him all she wants, two-time him for Simon. I don't care, just as long as she doesn't talk about him near me. And I do not want to hear about him and how he fancies me. It's just… gross.

Mum puts her mug to her lips, sipping her coffee. She smiles at me. "You can say that now, honey." She gets up from the table. "But you could end up falling for him."

I scoff. What makes my mum think I will eventually like him? I will never like him. I hated him. He is just the same as every other guy that makes me loathe them.

Mum turns to walk over to the sink. With her back to us, I stick my middle finger up at my sister. She does it in return.

I quickly stuffed the rest of my cereal into my mouth so I could get out of here. I didn't want to be asked more questions about Nathan. There was nothing to talk about him, but according to Lindsay, there was. Mum re-joins us at the table to finish her breakfast, and Lindsay resumes our conversation about Nathan, telling a thing or two about him to Mum.

I stand up from the table, not wanting to hear that jerk's name ever again. "Are we done talking about Nathan?"

When neither of them responds, I take my bowl over to the dishwasher and walk out of the kitchen to get ready for school. Thank goodness it's Friday.

Once I'm ready, I sit on the couch and sketch in my book while I wait for my sister to get ready. She takes her time, as if she had all day. Half of me wanted to leave her ass here and head to school without her. I almost left, but then she came down the stairs, telling me she was ready to go.

I drive us to school in silence with only the sound of the radio playing. Lindsay turns it up full blast. For a moment we squabble over how loud to have the music, and in the end Lindsay wins over it.

We go our separate ways once I park the car. Lindsay heads off somewhere with Emilynn. I have a free period this morning, and made my way to the library where I can be alone until second period.

I'm the only student in the library this morning, just the way I like it. I sit down at a table and draw in my sketchbook, continuing on the sketch of my dad and me at the beach that I worked on yesterday. The drawing is almost done, and I wanted to finish it today so I could move onto the next drawing.

My peace didn't last long when someone placed a pile of books down on the table in front of me. At first I thought it was the librarian, but no. It wasn't her at all. It was that idiot Nathan, helping himself to a seat in front of me. I frown at him. Who does he think he is, just helping himself to a seat at this table without my consent? I look around to see that we were the only students here. Out of all the other empty tables in here, he had to sit right here next to me?

Great. He just has to spend his free period here in the library. Why can't this guy just leave me alone for once and stop talking to me? I'm pretty sure he could stalk someone else. I mean, Lindsay is the one who fancies him. Why not stalk her?

"What are you doing here?" I ask, snapping my book closed.

"I saw you sitting by yourself so I thought–"

"You thought what? That you will come over here and annoy me?"

He shakes his head. "No. I just thought I will come join you and keep you company."

"Nathan, I don't need your company. I enjoy sitting here by myself."

"I'm sorry."

"Why are you stalking me? First you give me a rose for Valentine's, expecting me to accept, and what, go out with you? Then you asked my sister for our landline, calling me three times in a row. Now you're sitting at the same table as me. What else do you want?"

"I just want to be your friend."

Friend? He wants to be friends?

I put my pencil down, letting it sit on my sketchbook. It rolls off it, but I grab it, placing it back on the book again. I don't want to believe Nathan when he said he wanted to be friends. Why would I be the person he wants to be friends with? I mean, he likes me more than just a friend, doesn't he? So why lie to me? Is he afraid of what I will say? Because he definitely should be afraid.

"What do you see in me?" I ask. "Can't you find someone else to like?"

Nathan shakes his head. "Maybe I could like someone else, but I don't want to." He looks me straight in the eye. When he does, it sends shivers down my spine because whatever he says means he is telling the truth. "I like you, Alex. I think you're beautiful, smart, and you don't let anyone stand in your way. You're different to other girls in our grade. And I know your sister fancies me, but she isn't you, Alex. In fact, you don't chase me like she does, and you're definitely harder to read."

My stomach ties into knots, or maybe it's butterflies. I'm not entirely sure. I can't exactly explain how I feel since butterflies are not something I have experience before. His blue eyes never leave mine. He wasn't lying about how he felt about me. I stare back at him, trying to decide whether

I should really believe him. For a moment, I consider believing him. No guy has ever said that to me before. But then again, every single guy on Earth would say those words to any girl they come across. Playing with their hearts to get what they want and then stabbing them later. It may not happen to everyone, but being in love is full of heartbreaks that always leave you disappointed. What is stopping Nathan from doing the same thing to me? I don't want to be used just for Nathan's own pleasure.

I have to go. I can't stand to stay here any longer with Nathan. Standing up from my seat, I gather up my stuff. Hopefully I can find a new location without Nathan around to bother me.

"Why don't you like anyone being around you?" Nathan asks me, watching me gather up my stuff.

"It's because I like to be alone."

"Nobody likes to be alone, Alex. Not even an introvert does. In our lives, we all would like to be surrounded by someone."

I scoff. Did he seriously think that? I'm not like everyone else. I'd rather be by myself than with people who eventually leave you. It's better to be alone than to get hurt.

"Wow, you really know nothing about me then," I tell him.

I stand up from the table and walk towards the exit. Nathan follows me.

I spin around to face him, frowning. "Why are you still stalking me?"

"I want you to give me a chance," he says. "I want us to be friends. We don't have to be lovers, just friends."

He's unbelievable. Clearly threatening him over the phone yesterday, or shoving him the other day, hasn't helped. What do I need to do to make him understand how I don't like anyone, nor do I want to be friends with anyone? The last friend I had ditched me for a new friend group when we went to different high schools. I haven't had a friend since I was twelve, and I don't need any friends now. It just saves me from being hurt by being ditched by someone else. What's stopping Nathan from befriending me, only to end the friendship once he grew bored with me? Besides, I'm not like my sister. I'm not exactly great at making friends. Lindsay is an extrovert, always knowing how to socialise with people. I don't know how.

And what hurts the most about losing my friend is that she was the one I shared my thoughts on my dad leaving. Perhaps she grew tired of listening to me talk about him. There was Mum and Lindsay I could talk to, but sometimes I felt talking to a friend was better. Clearly it wasn't because they just didn't care about me.

"Did you not listen to one word I told you back there?" I ask him.

"Alex, I–"

"Leave me alone, you jerk." I hurry out of the library.

I head towards the shelter area. I glance behind me to make sure Nathan isn't following me, and thankfully he isn't. Good. He got the message.

Hopefully.

Chapter 11

Thankfully for the rest of the morning, I don't see Nathan in the halls as I head off to second period. I get lucky and don't see him at recess or the other two periods. When the bell rings for lunch, I make my way through the crowd in hope my luck is still there. Can I get through the day without seeing him after this morning? Probably not, but I'm going to try to.

I keep my focus ahead as I hurry to the shelter area before it fills up, not wanting to look around in case I spot Nathan. But instead of seeing him, I see my sister. Lindsay is standing under a tree, kissing Simon. I roll my eyes. Did she seriously have to be doing that right there for everyone to see?

I hope she gets busted by a teacher.

I walk over to them, grabbing Lindsay's arm and pull her away from Simon. If I didn't do that, I'm sure a teacher would have, so they better be thankful that I have just saved them from detention.

Or maybe I should have let them get caught. They should both know that kissing was against the school rules.

Lindsay twirls around, pushing my hand away. She frowns when she sees it's me.

"What on earth, Alex! What is your problem?" she demanded.

"Yes, bitch. What is your problem?" Simon imitates my sister.

I ignore him, keeping my focus on my sister. "I'm sorry if I have just saved your ass from being caught by a teacher and getting detention. Besides, no one wants to see you make out with your boyfriend."

Lindsay rolls her eyes. "Relax, Alex. I'm not going to get caught by a teacher. Simon and I kiss all the time on the school grounds."

"Well, someone will catch you one of these days. It's against school rules, Lindsay. Also, show some respect. Not everyone wants to see you make out with Simon."

Simon steps forward, frowning. "You're telling Lindsay to have some respect?" He scoffs. "Oh, Alex Jennings. You should speak for yourself. You never show respect to others, and you're always telling people what they should do. Then you complain how much you hate everyone. Are you jealous or something that Lindsay has an amazing boyfriend?"

I narrow my eyes at him. Did he really have to get involved?

"I agree with Simon," Lindsay says. "I mean, the last time I checked, you were the one who needed to show respect. Like, how about not telling me what to do for once? Or stop thinking you're Little Miss Perfect who is against the world and can't do anything wrong?"

I clench my jaw. "Well, at least I know I'm not a slut."

She narrows her eyes at me, and then shoves me hard in the chest. "Never call me that again!"

I return the shove. "Stop pushing."

"No, I will do whatever I want!" She shoves me. "Stop telling me what to do!"

We keep pushing each other, spitting insults at each other. Simon isn't doing anything to stop us from fighting. He's recording our fight on his phone. Lindsay grabs my hair and pulls on it. I squeal, and then whack her in the jaw. She stumbles back, and I elbow her in the stomach.

Students nearby are now gathering around to see what is going on. They began egging us on rather than trying to stop us from fighting. Some are coping Simon and pulling out their phones to record.

Our fight doesn't last long when someone yells, "That's enough."

Lindsay's photography teacher, Mr Fraser, gets in between us, holding out his arms to stop us from fighting more.

Mr Fraser marches us to the principal's office. Mr Matthews will not be pleased to see me again after only just seeing me in his office earlier this week.

***

It wasn't a surprise for Mr Matthews to see me in his office, as I'm one of his regulars who is always being sent to him for "disrupting the peace". But it is a surprise for him to see my sister, though. She has never been in trouble for anything.

Until now.

He watches my sister and me as we bicker in his office, putting the blame on each other for why we are in the principal's office.

Mr Matthews steps in, doing his best to calm us down. But no matter what he did, we kept bickering, explaining to him what had happened. In the end, he thought it was best to send us home, calling Mum. He also issues us with an afternoon detention for tomorrow.

"I can't believe I have to leave work early to come pick you girls up," Mum scolds as we follow her out of the office.

"Alex started it," Lindsay spits out, immediately blaming me. "She is the one who pushed me first!"

"Like I said, you should have some respect for people," I say.

"Wow, that's incredibly hilarious coming from your own mouth when you don't even do the same thing."

"Girls, give it a rest," Mum stops us before we can get into another catfight. "I don't care who started what. I don't need you to act like seven-year-olds. If you ask me, you both should learn some respect. You both need to sort out your differences."

Whatever. Lindsay deserved it. I'm not even sorry for starting the fight.

Behind Mum's back, Lindsay turns to me and sticks up her middle finger. I return the gesture.

We follow Mum out of the school entrance, turning left, and head down the street. "Girls, I would like you to be on your best behaviour for the rest of the afternoon. I don't care what problems you have between each other; I just don't want any trouble tonight. If you have a problem with something, I want you to keep your comments to yourself. Dereck is coming over for dinner tonight."

I roll my eyes. "Seriously? He was over here yesterday! He has been coming around for dinner a lot lately. Doesn't he know how to cook for himself? He is acting like he lives with us."

"Alex, I don't have time to listen to your complaints about Dereck," she scolds. "He is my guest, and I have invited him. Please, just keep your comments about him to yourself and be nice to him. I don't want you girls to be fighting anymore." Mum stops in front of her car that is parked under a tree. "I want you to control your anger, Alex. And just to make sure that you girls don't end up killing each other, I want Lindsay to come home with me. Alex, you can drive your car home."

Lindsay groans. "Seriously? Alex gets the car? Why can't I drive it for once?"

"Just get in the car, Lindsay," Mum says in a firm voice.

Obeying Mum, she gets into the front seat of the car once Mum unlocks it. Without a word to my mother, I push past her and continue to walk down the street towards my car. I heard the engine of my mother's car starting up and driving away. I don't look back at her, but something makes me turn to my left. When I do, I see Nathan standing beside the fence of the playing field, eating a sandwich as he watches me. His friend Eric isn't with him. I stand there, staring back at him. How did he know I was out here?

Normally I would have stormed over to him, demanding to know why he was stalking me, but I didn't feel like doing anything to him this time.

After staring at him for a few minutes, I was the first to break eye contact and continue walking down the street until I came to my car. I unlock it, throwing my bag into the passenger seat. I sit there for a moment, wondering whether Nathan had followed me or was he already standing at the fence before I came out. Why is he even standing there in the first place? Is he trying to make fun of me for being sent home for the day?

I still wonder what he even sees in me. I'm not someone he should like. Can he just forget about me?

Chapter 12

I haven't left my room since arriving home. Nor have I spoken a word to my sister or Mum. The only time I left my room was to head downstairs for something to drink. Mum is in the kitchen cooking dinner. We hardly made any eye contact or said two words to each other. Mum only informs me that dinner was almost ready.

That means idiot Dereck will be here soon.

Leaving Mum with my can of Coke in my hand, I headed back to my room. On my way back, I walked past my sister's room. She's talking on the phone when I walk past, mentioning my name. I press my ear against the door, eavesdropping on Lindsay's conversation, of which I could only hear one side. I don't know who she was speaking to, but my guess is it was Emilynn.

"You know, I don't get it with Alex," Lindsay says. "She is just plain weird. How on earth can you hate everything and everyone? She doesn't even have a reason to dislike everyone. She got me into trouble for nothing. All I did was kiss Simon. There was no reason for her to tell me I couldn't kiss on the school grounds. She isn't a teacher. Sometimes I don't know why we're twins. We don't even act like we are."

My stomach felt like Lindsay's words had kicked me in the stomach as I turn away from the door. I may dislike my sister, but how could she even question why we are twins? Did she really doubt being my sister, or was she only saying it to Emilynn? I can't help that we are twins. All twins are different, even if we aren't acting like we are. We are still sisters, and nothing can ever change that.

And she is wrong about me for not having a reason to hate everyone and everything. I have a reason. I loathed everyone to protect myself from being hurt when I get close to someone, just in case they leave me. Like Dad did. I couldn't get hurt if I hated everyone. I also loathed everything because most things reminded me of my dad.

I'm about to move away from the door when I hear Lindsay mention Nathan's name. I press my ear back against the door, curious to know what she has to say about him this time. It was hard to know what Emilynn was saying as I could only hear one side of the conversation, but still I wondered what she might be saying. Was she saying something good about Nathan, or was it all bad? Whatever they were talking about, Lindsay mostly wanted to know what Nathan did once we left the school.

The doorbell rings at that moment. I move away from the door before I get caught standing there. Dereck. He just has to show up now. Why can't he go away and leave my family alone?

Making my way over to the stairs, I hear my mother open the door and greet Dereck. From the top of the stairs, I see Mum give him a kiss. I hid behind the wall so they wouldn't see me watching them.

"Lindsay, Alex, come on down," Mum calls. "Dereck is here."

I don't move. I don't want to. Not if I have to see his face. I think back to the other night when he asked me if I wanted to go to an art exhibition with him. What is he going to do tonight to get me to like him?

Taking a deep breath, I force myself to join my mother and her boyfriend downstairs. Dereck smiles at me when I turn from behind the wall. I don't return the smile. Mum glances at me, giving me a look to tell me I need to be nice. Why should I even bother to be nice?

Lindsay pushes past me, knocking me into the wall. Mum sees her do it and warns her not to do anything that will cause me to be mad. Lindsay doesn't apologise. Instead, she greets Dereck happily. He returns the greeting.

I continue down the rest of the stairs, hanging onto the banister. Dereck greets me and offers to give me a hug, but I step back. He gets the message and puts his hands up in apology. Mum tells us dinner is ready. We follow her into the kitchen and take our usual seats at the table. Mum serves us our food, humming happily to herself. What's up with Mum tonight? She never hums while serving us dinner.

The meatloaf Mum made smells good. I pick up my knife and fork to tuck into the meal when Mum speaks.

"Before we eat, Dereck and I would like to make an announcement," Mum announces excitedly.

I feel my stomach twist into knots. The last time Mum was excited about something was when she first came home to introduce us to Dereck. What could be more exciting than dating him?

"Something we think you both might like," Dereck adds. He looks in my direction. I bite down on my lip as I narrow my eyes at him, preventing me from saying anything and getting into an argument with Mum. "Well, what one of you might like. I'm sure you will like it too, Alex, even though you won't show it."

I scoff. "I doubt it."

Mum smiles at Dereck and then reaches across the table. Dereck meets her hand halfway and interlaces it with his. I stare at their hands. Something on my mum's finger of her left hand catches my eye. It's a silver ring that I've never seen before. Is that new? My stomach no longer twists. It feels like it's stabbing itself. No, she can't be. How can she?

"Mum, what is that?" I ask, glancing up at her. "Is that a ring?"

Mum's smile grows wider. "Girls, as you know, it has been six months since Dereck and I have been dating. Two nights ago Dereck proposed to me. I said yes. We are planning to get married maybe in July over your winter break."

My heart pounds fast in my chest while my head spins, taking in all of this information. No. This can't be happening. Mum can't be engaged to this loser. What about Dad? What if he comes back? How can she allow Dereck to walk into our family and take over like he has always been a part of it?

Lindsay cheers. "Congratulations."

I shake my head. No. This can't be happening. Mum and Dereck can't get married. Suddenly, I find myself unable to breathe.

Mum notices me struggling to breathe. She gets up, asking me if I'm alright.

"You can't get married!" I burst out.

Mum freezes where she is, half standing. Dereck and Lindsay turn to me, their eyes widening from my sudden outburst.

"What do you mean I can't get married, honey?" Mum asks, sitting back down in her chair.

Lindsay rolls her eyes at me. "Let me guess. You hate weddings."

Ignoring my sister, I keep my focus on my mother. "Mum, you can't get married! You just can't! You didn't even ask us if you could get married." I turn to Dereck, narrowing my eyes at him. "And you should have asked Lindsay and me if this is what we wanted. We don't need a second dad."

Lindsay rolls her eyes. "What do you mean he needs to ask us? He doesn't need to ask us. He's a grown man, stupid."

Mum gives Lindsay a stern look. "Lindsay." She turns her focus back to me, and calmly says, "Alex, it has been almost seven years since your father had walked out. He ended our marriage. He is never coming back. Since meeting Dereck, he has helped me to move on from your father."

My heart crumbles in my chest. What does Mum mean he isn't coming back? He needs to return. "Of course he is coming back!"

Though I know deep inside, Mum is right. Dad is never coming back. He left us. He doesn't want us. Still, I wanted to hold on to the hope that he would return.

I get up, not caring that I have knocked my chair over as it crashes to the floor. I ran out of the kitchen and out the front door. No one tries to stop me from running. Mum doesn't even call after me.

I run down the street, heading to Wakefield Park, which is two blocks away from our house. Lindsay and I used to play there all the time with Dad. I still go there, usually just to think, draw, or whenever I want to be alone. Tears spill hard down my cheeks. Mum can't get married. Why hasn't Dad returned home yet? He could put a stop to this wedding. He has to. Even when Mum told Lindsay that he wasn't coming back, I didn't believe her. I believe he will return someday. I know they divorced, but Dad is still a part of this family for crying out loud! He could come home and change his mind about everything, beg mum to take him back so we could be a happy family again.

I don't slow to stop, not even to look both ways crossing the road. I didn't care if a car were to suddenly come out of nowhere and hit me. No one will care if I am hit by a car. My chest feels like exploding as I keep pushing myself to run, not caring if I were to drop dead from a heart attack. I'm almost at the park, and I can rest there. No one will think to look for me there. And even if they know where to find me, I don't want to speak to Mum or Lindsay. I especially don't want to talk to Dereck. I will not let that jerk walk into our family and take over!

I'm blinded by my own tears as they make my vision blurry. I'm unable to see where I'm going until I crash into something. Well someone. I quickly wipe my eyes so I can see who I'd crashed into. It was a guy walking his dog. I don't look to see who it is. I only saw his chest, but never looked to see who was wearing the sky-blue t-shirt and black jeans.

"Hey," he says.

The voice sounds familiar, and when I glance up, I see that it's Nathan Bridges. Great, just the person I don't want to see. Don't tell me he lives around this area? I push past Nathan, not wanting to stop and talk to him. I need to get out of here and clear my head.

I move around him, but before I had the chance to run again, Nathan grabs my wrist, pulling me back towards him.

"Alex, what's wrong?" he asks.

I push Nathan away from me, making him let go of my wrist, but he wouldn't. He tightens his grip on me. "Let go of me, you jerk!"

Nathan lets go of the dog leash and grabs both of my arms with his hands. He makes me face him, gripping my arms so I couldn't slip away from him. Doesn't he understand me when I told him to leave me alone?

"Alex, tell me what's wrong."

My eyes widened at his words. No way could I tell him what was wrong. Why would he care how I feel?

I shake my head, trying to break free. I couldn't. Nathan had a firm grip on my wrist.

"Leave me alone! I don't need your help!"

"Alex, whatever the problem is, I will listen to you."

I stop struggling and stare at Nathan. I can't see him. The tears have blurred my vision once again. He was serious when he said he wanted to listen to me. I can hear it in his voice. It's gentle, just like Miss Giovanni's voice. I don't find many people whose voices are gentle. No one ever wanted to listen to my problems, except for Miss Giovanni. Sure, people always said to me they would listen, but I knew truthfully they wouldn't really care. They will just tell me to get over it. Miss Giovanni never forced me to talk if I didn't want to. She always lets me talk when I feel like I was ready. That's how Nathan sounded. I never noticed how gentle his voice was until now.

Nathan curses, dropping my arms, and runs after his dog, who has taken off. I hear a dog bark and some ducks quacking. The dog chases the ducks that hang around the park where a creek is nearby. I quickly wipe the tears away from my eyes and stare at Nathan as he ran after his dog, which he called Lou. This was the perfect chance to make my escape before Nathan came after me, but instead of running away, I ran over to Nathan to help him catch his dog.

Lou thought it was a game as we chased him. He doesn't even want to stop. My chest is getting ready to explode since I didn't have a proper rest before, but I keep pushing myself on. I finally caught Lou by stepping onto his leash after so many tries of stepping on it so Lou couldn't run. I grab the leash off the grass. Nathan runs over to me and stands in front of me, breathless. For a moment we stand there in silence, staring at each other while we catch our breath.

"Thanks," Nathan finally says, panting, taking the leash from me. "I didn't expect you would help me chase after Lou."

"Yeah, well, if I didn't help you then you will chase your dog all afternoon," I panted.

"Thank you."

We stand there in silence again. Nathan stares at me, but I stare at the ground instead. Lou's a beagle, and I watch him sit by Nathan's feet, panting.

"Hey, would you like to hang out for a while?" Nathan continues. "You know, as friends? I won't ask you out. I promise, Alex. Maybe we can talk and you can tell me what's bothering you."

I glance up at him, his eyes soft and caring. Why is he being so nice to me, especially when I'm always rude to him? And why would he want to hear about my problems?

I look around to see if anyone from school was in the park. The last thing I wanted was to be caught hanging out with Nathan. There's no one here besides us, so I guess that is a good thing.

I turn back to Nathan. "I guess so. But if anyone from school sees us, don't expect me to be very nice to you."

Nathan leads us over to a bench looking out onto the playground. He sits Lou on his lap, and for a moment we sit there in silence.

"How old is he?" I ask.

"He is almost two years old." Nathan scratches behind Lou's ears. Lou has his tongue out and what looks like a smile. "So, do you want to talk about why you have been crying? Is everything okay?"

I sigh. I can't believe I'm about to tell him this. "My mum is getting married to some moron."

Nathan's eyes widened at my choice of words. "I see. Shouldn't you be happy she is getting married?"

I shake my head. "No, I'm not. I don't want her to remarry. I want everything to go back to the way it was when my dad was around."

"Is it okay to ask what happened to your dad?"

I don't answer him straight away. Should I tell him? Or should I shut him out? He doesn't need to know anything about my dad or anything about my personal life.

I feel his eyes on me, waiting for me to answer him. I don't have to tell him about my dad, do I? No. He doesn't need to know. No one needs to know anything about him. It's no one's business.

"Nathan, I just want to say that I'm sorry about the other day," I say, changing the subject. I nervously twist my bracelets before glancing up at him. "You know, for embarrassing you in front of the class when you handed me the rose. I shouldn't have done that."

Nathan looks at me, his eyes widening. "Are you actually apologising to me? I heard you don't apologise to anyone."

He is right. I don't apologise. Why am I apologising to Nathan for what I did?

"I don't know why. It just slipped out of my mouth."

"Can I ask you something? Why do you dislike everyone?"

I don't answer Nathan straight away. Discussing my past with him is not something I feel comfortable with. I don't even feel comfortable talking to Miss Giovanni about it. Why was I even talking to Nathan in the first place?

"I don't want to tell you the reason," I answer. "You wouldn't understand. No one does. You will make fun of me for that reason."

Nathan shakes his head. "I won't make fun of you. I promise."

"That's what everyone says. If I tell anyone, they will say I'm not normal. Lindsay always says I'm not normal."

"Lindsay doesn't know what she is talking about. I mean, we all have a reason for something. It doesn't mean we aren't normal."

Nathan was right. My sister didn't know what she was talking about, even though she thought she did. From the day Dad walked out, and I punished everyone for him leaving, Lindsay said I wasn't normal. I'm sure everyone thinks the same way she does. It didn't make me comfortable to open up about how I felt about my dad with the things she said. And even when I'm forced to see Miss Giovanni, I hate the idea of revealing everything to her. What does she truly think of me, even when she says she wants to help?

I sit in silence. I can't tell Nathan everything. Even if he wants to listen.

When I don't speak, Nathan does. "You know, I totally get it if you don't want your mum to remarry. I was the same when both of my parents remarried after they divorced. It sucks. It really does. But the main thing is that they are happy together. At least be happy for your mum, even if you aren't."

I look at him, unaware that Nathan's parents divorced. But then again, I know nothing about him. He said to be happy for Mum, yet how can I when I'm not happy myself?

Nathan lifts Lou off his lap and places him on the grass.

"I should get going, Alex," he tells me. "I will see you in school."

He gets up, grabbing the dog leash, and starts walking away.

Damn it, Alex. Why don't you open up to him? He said he would listen. You may never get another chance. If his parents had divorced, he would understand what you are going through.

Before I can talk myself out of anything, I get off the grass, chasing after Nathan.

"Nathan, wait!"

Nathan stops and turns to me.

"All of those things you said about listening, do you mean it?" I ask as I stand in front of him.

Nathan gives me a small smile. "Of course. Whenever you are ready to talk, we can talk."

"Okay, well in that case, I will open up to you once I get to know you. Maybe we could spend time with each other. Like hang out." The words were out of my mouth before I even knew what I was doing. Was spending time with Nathan a good idea? I cross my arms across my chest. "On a date. If I enjoy it, then I'll let you take me out more often. But I will only go out with you on one condition: Do not tell anyone about the date. Not even your friend Eric. If anyone finds out about us, don't expect me to be nice to you."

Nathan smiles. "Okay. The date will be our little secret." He zips his mouth.

We made plans for Monday night, where he already had something planned that he said I'll love. I doubt I would, but I agree to go along with whatever he has planned. Maybe he will prove me wrong, and I'll enjoy it. Miss Giovanni wants me to open up and trust people. This is one way to start, right? Forcing myself to go on a date with a guy I do not know if I like, but he does like me.

And this is the first step that I, Alexander Madeline Jennings, need to make in order to open up to others. Even if the whole time I'd rather keep a distance from the others. But sometimes you can't.

Chapter 13

I don't head home straight away, not until it's near sunset.
I narrow my eyes, clenching my fists together when I see
Dereck's black Honda parked on the street. What makes
him think he has the right to just walk into my family? I
will show him exactly how I feel about him. Walking over
to the driver's side, I look up at the house, making sure
Mum or Dereck weren't looking through the window.
Even if they were, I don't care. I kick the driver's door as
hard as I could, making a small dent. I groan as pain shot
up through my toe, but I shake the pain off. Smiling to
myself, I wonder what Dereck will say when he sees the
dent. Would he know I did it?

I limp to the footpath. Before making my way up the
lawn, I lean up on Dereck's car to wait for the throbbing
in my toe to subside. When the pain is gone, I walk inside,
opening the front door to find the lounge room empty. I
thought of heading to the kitchen to eat my dinner that I
hadn't touched, but I decided not to. Even if my stomach
grumbled with hunger, I knew Dereck would be in there.

I don't want to see his face. Seeing him will just make me madder than I already am.

And even if I could say something nasty to make him want to leave, he wouldn't go. He will stay here. Why should a seventeen-year-old girl scare him off for marrying the woman he loves, even if one of his future stepdaughters dislikes him?

"Alex, is that you?" Mum calls from the kitchen.

Instead of responding, I run up the stairs and hid in my room before Mum could see me, slamming the door shut behind me. I switch on my CD player that Lindsay told me to get rid of so many times, telling me it's outdated, but I don't care. Music is all I need right now to calm me down. An annoying pop song comes onto the radio that I keep hearing constantly being played repeatedly. I let out a small, frustrating scream, switching off the horrible song.

Maybe quiet is all I needed right now. I just need to get my sketchbook and I should be fine.

As soon as I sit down on my bed, there's a knock at the door. My mother's voice follows, asking if she can come in so we can talk.

I roll my eyes, getting off the bed. I know exactly what she wanted to talk about. She wasn't coming in here to see how I was. No, the conversation will be about Dereck, the wedding, and how I should get over my dad who was never coming back. I don't want to talk about any of that. All I want is to be alone right now. Mum will never understand how I feel. It's not about what I wanted. It was all about her and what she wants. She doesn't care about me. She doesn't even care about Dad. All she cares about is Dereck.

Instead of opening the door, I switch the CD player back on. The same annoying pop song comes back on. No matter how much I disliked the song, I turn the volume up loud so I couldn't hear Mum calling me. I walk over to my bed and sit down, grabbing my sketchbook from under my pillow. Getting comfortable, I open to a clean page of my sketchbook and begin drawing.

The door swings open, where Mum had somehow picked the lock. I groan. Did the "Do not disturb" sign on my door not mean anything? What is the point of it being there if everyone was going to ignore it? I watch her from the corner of my eye as she closed the door behind her. The first thing she does is switch off the CD player before making her way over to me. I quickly closed my sketchbook before Mum sees what I'm drawing and set it on the bed beside me.

I don't dare to make eye contact with my mother.

"We need to talk, Alex," she says in a calm voice, letting me know she didn't want to argue.

I force myself to look at her. "No, we don't. Even if I express my feelings, you wouldn't care less about what I think of you getting remarried to Dereck."

Mum shakes her head. "I do care, Alex." She sits down on the edge of my bed, facing me. "Look, I know you never liked me dating again. And at first I wasn't sure if it was something I should do after your father left. But I really liked Dereck, and didn't want to lose out on the opportunity to get to know him. I understand how you feel about Dereck. But I also need you to understand me, Alex, with how Dereck has made me feel since I met him. He has made me happy. He made me feel loved again since losing your father. I know he can never replace your father, but I want you and Lindsay to be happy too."

"Well, I'm not happy. Maybe you and Lindsay are glad to have Dereck part of this family, don't expect me to be happy too. He doesn't belong in this family. Dad does. He is still a part of the family. How can you even think about getting with for another man?"

Mum takes a deep breath before exhaling it slowly, trying to keep calm. "Alex, I know you want your father back. But he is never returning home. He left us."

I cross my arms across my chest, frowning. "How do you know he won't come back?"

"He left us, Alex. He wrote it in a letter because he was too much of a coward to say it to my face. Or to tell you girls how he no longer wanted you."

My heart sinks at the thought of Dad not wanting me or my sister. Am I to blame for why he left? Or Lindsay? Or was there another reason he left? Still, I wonder what if he were to return, realising his mistake for leaving us? "And you think it's right to date another man?"

Mum stares at me, biting her lip. There are tears forming in her eyes, but she doesn't let them fall. She stands up from my bed. "You know, Alex, I really do not know what your problem is. You really have to think about others. This universe does not revolve around you. I don't care what you have to say, but you have no right to be speaking to me like that or to anyone. I know Dereck isn't your father, but the least you can do is show a little respect for him. It has been almost seven years since your father and I divorced. He isn't coming back, Alex. He left his family."

"Liar. He is coming back."

"No. It's the truth, Alex. You need to realise that. He never promised you he would come back. I wish I could tell you he will, but he never said goodbye to any of us. He is gone, Alex. Whatever anger you have towards him, let it go. Stop treating everyone like crap."

I open my mouth to say something, but decided not to. It was better if I said nothing. Mum understands nothing about how I feel about Dad.

Once she leaves the room, the tears build up again. I lay on my bed, hugging my sketchbook close to my chest. Dad is going to come back. I know he is. He loves me, doesn't he? Why did he leave?

***

I thought I could stay in my room all night, drawing in my sketchbook, but eventually I couldn't ignore the grumbling in my stomach. Putting the book aside, I head downstairs.

Someone was in the shower when I passed the upstairs bathroom, and I wanted to hope it was Mum so I couldn't cross her. It was quiet downstairs. It was like no one was around at all as I made my way to the kitchen. Maybe Dereck has gone home?

He hasn't. Dereck was clearing the dishwasher when I entered the kitchen.

Without saying a word to him, I walk over to the fridge where I find my plate. I place it in the microwave. With the silence between us, I can feel Dereck's eyes on me as I wait in front of the microwave for my food.

Dereck wipes a plate with a towel and then set it down on the counter. "Alex, can we talk?"

I roll my eyes, crossing my arms across my chest. I turn to face him. "No. I don't want to talk to you."

"Alex, I know you don't like me because you might think I'm taking over your father. I promise you I'm not."

"Whatever."

"I know I can never replace your father, Alex."

"Good. I don't want you to replace him."

The microwave beeps. I take out my dinner and set it down on the table. Dereck hands me a knife and fork. I snatch it from him without saying thank you.

"Can we work this out, Alex?" he asks me as I sit down at the table.

I ignore him, stuffing meatloaf into my mouth so I don't have to speak.

Dereck sits down in the chair next to me. He rests his hand on my arm, but I shake it away, giving him a warning look not to touch me again.

"All I ask you to do is give me a chance, Alex."

I swallow quickly. "Why should I?"

"I love your mother. I want to make her happy, as well as you and Lindsay. Instead of thinking of me as another father figure in your life, why not think of me as a friend?"

"I don't want to be friends with you. Can you just leave me alone and let me eat dinner in peace?"

He nods, his eyes filled with disappointment with his attempt to make conversation with me. Why does he even try when he knows I want nothing to do with him? He can't force me to like him. I don't need another father figure in my life.

Respecting my wishes, Dereck walks back over to the dishwasher and finishes loading it. Once he has done that, he leaves the kitchen. Good. I am alone at last.

Chapter 14

For the rest of the evening, Mum and I don't speak. It was all for the best that we didn't. I stayed in my room to avoid both her and Dereck. But there was one time I did sneak downstairs to get a drink, and I heard the two of them talking in the lounge room. They talk quietly about the wedding, about Dad, and about me. I stand where they couldn't hear or see me, listening to everything they say.

"I love my daughters, Dereck," Mum had said. "I want what is best for them. They were twelve when their father walked out of the lives. Lindsay and Alex don't deserve that. Now I feel Alex hates me for wanting to get remarried. She still believes her father will come back into our lives, but I don't know how to break it to her that he won't. I don't even know where he is."

Dereck puts his arms around Mum, snuggling her. "It's okay, Jean. I know this is a big step for the girls. But I promise you that everything is going to work out fine. As for Alex, I'm sure in time she will accept your decision."

I don't dare to enter the lounge room to get my drink because I knew the conversation would turn over to me. I stand there listening for a bit before heading back to my room. My heart crumbles in my chest. All around me I feel like the world is ending, and I'm caught in between. I should be happy for my mother finding someone who loves her and is there for her, just like how Dad was. But I didn't want it to be with another man. I wanted it to be with Dad. I want everything to go back to how it used to be when we were a family of four.

But it never will. How do I accept Dereck being a part of our lives when I don't want him to?

In the morning, to avoid Mum, I sneak down early to eat something before heading back up to my room. I figured Mum would avoid talking too after the argument last night, but when she called me downstairs Saturday morning, it was like last night never happened, and she was speaking to me normally.

She hands me the phone, smiling. "It's Nathan calling."

I roll my eyes when I take the phone from her. Of course, it is. No one else is going to call me on a Saturday morning.

What does Nathan want now? I think to myself. Just because we spoke at the park yesterday, it doesn't mean I want him to call me up over the weekend. It doesn't mean I like him even if I agreed to allow him to take me out on Monday night.

I wait for Mum to leave before I speak. "What do you want, Nathan?"

"Hey," Nathan says. "Sorry to be calling you when I know you said you don't want me calling here, but I want to know what you are doing today?"

I blink for a moment. He called just to ask me that? "Why do you want to know?"

"My uncle is the manager at Splash Resort, and I was wondering if you would like to come to the park with me?"

I raise my eyebrows. "Seriously? A water park?"

"Yeah, it will be great."

I groan. "No. I hate Splash Resort."

"What is there to hate about it? Come on, Alex. Who can say no to a water slide?"

"No. I'm not interested."

"Alex, come on. Come join me at the park. It will be fun. It will just be you and me."

I roll my eyes, sighing. I hate this guy. Why does he try so hard to impress me when he knows very well that I'm not interested? Thankfully Lindsay was spending the day with Emilynn, and she couldn't eavesdrop on my conversation with Nathan. I could imagine getting off the phone and having my sister call me a freak because I wouldn't go out with Nathan.

"Nathan, just because you asked me out for Monday does not mean I want to spend the weekend with you either."

"I know. But I figure where I want to take you on Monday, we might not pay so much attention to each other. So I thought we could go to Splash Resort where it's a much better place for us to hang out and get to know each other. Let's not make it a date. We will make it like a friends' day out. What do you say?"

Why must he ask me? "Why can't you go with Eric? He's your friend."

"I would, but he's busy today. Besides, you are my friend too, Alex. Come join me, please."

I sigh. I might as well say yes, or he will never stop begging me to go with him. Or he will find another activity for us. I hope I don't regret this. "Fine. I will go. But if anyone from school is there, we pretend we aren't there together."

I feel his smile through the phone. Even if I couldn't see it, the butterflies danced around my stomach at the thought of hanging out with him.

I tell him to meet me at the park. The last thing I wanted was Mum asking me questions about whose car I was getting into.

Mum walks into the lounge room, a smile crossing her lips. "What did Nathan want? Are you planning to go out?"

I turn to Mum, unsure how to explain to her where I was going on a Saturday with a boy. Knowing that she may have heard the conversation, and the guilt of sneaking around so no one sees me with Nathan was like being caught for doing something I shouldn't. I could tell Mum where I was going, but I wanted to avoid the questions. What will she think of me hanging out with Nathan? "Yeah, I'm going out for a bit. I will be back later. I don't know how long I will be."

Mum's smile grew. "That's great, Alex. Where are you two going?"

My brain panics with a thousand things running through my head, terrified of what my mother will say about me going out to a water park with a guy from school. What will she think? What would she say? Am I brave enough to reveal my plans to her?

"I'm just going to the park." I mean, it's not completely a lie.

Mum gives me a knowing smile. "Are you going on a date with Nathan?"

My eyes widen. "No. I am not. We are just hanging out as friends."

I run up to my room before Mum could ask me anymore questions. Would she think I'm going on an actual date? I didn't want her to make a fuss over it when that I didn't see Nathan as anything. He wasn't my friend and most definitely wasn't my boyfriend. All I was going to do was spend the day with him. Nothing else. And I hope Nathan understands that this wasn't a date.

I can't believe I'm agreeing to do this. I don't remember the last time I even wore a swimsuit, let alone went swimming. Not even when we had the school swimming carnival. I searched through the drawers, not remembering where I had put my swimsuit. Maybe if I tell Nathan that I no longer own one, he might change his mind about the water park.

I sneak back downstairs, carefully opening the hallway closet. I pull out a beach towel, and then head out the door, making my way towards the park. Wearing my baby-blue cap and sunglasses with pink lenses, I hope no one recognises me on the street.

I don't have to wait long for Nathan. He pulls up to the kerb five minutes after I had arrived. He smiles when he sees me, unlocking the door. I glance around me, making sure no one I knew was around, and climb into the front seat.

"Hi, Alex," Nathan greets me.

"Just so you know, I don't have a swimsuit," I say instead of returning the greeting, taking off my cap and sunglasses, placing them on my lap. "Well, I do. Somewhere. I couldn't find it. It's been a long time since I last went swimming."

"No worries, Alex. You can get one at the gift shop."

My heart sank deep in my chest as I rest the towel on my lap. Of course I could get one at the gift shop. So much for trying to get out of this. Why does Nathan even want me to come along with him?

"Since I invited you, I'll pay for the swimsuit," Nathan offers. "I will also pay for your entry."

I stare at him, speechless. No one has ever offered to do that for me. I mean, I act like a bitch to everyone, so of course no one would offer to do something like this. "You don't need to do that, Nathan. I can pay for it myself."

"It's okay." He smiles. "It's my treat, Alex."

I force myself to smile at him.

He turns on his indicator, looking over his shoulder before pulling away from the kerb.

I waited until we were halfway down the street before I said, "Thanks for inviting me. No one has ever invited me anywhere before."

"Well, can you blame them for not inviting you? I mean, everyone is afraid of you."

He has a point. I'm not complaining that no one asks me to do something with them because I'd rather be alone.

And I still can't believe I'm agreeing to go out with Nathan. I want to kick myself. What on earth is wrong with me?

"How come you aren't afraid of me?" I ask.

He turns to look at me for a second and then turns back to the road. "I don't know. There is something different about you that I like. I think there is a lot more to you than what people think. They know you as the girl who hates everything and everyone. But no one is looking to see the real you. And that's what I'm trying to find. The real you."

The real me. How is he supposed to find the real me when I don't even know the real me? I don't even know how I should respond. Is it supposed to be a compliment? Or is that something all guys say so you will like them in return? I can't tell.

The twenty minute drive to the park was mainly silent besides small talk. Nathan finds parking in the back of the lot. As we walk to the entrance, a nauseous feeling appears in the pit of my stomach. I glance around me, so sure that we were going to bump into someone we knew. I almost jumped out of my skin when I heard someone call out the name Lindsay, thinking that my sister was here. What do I do if it were her? But when I looked in the direction to see who it was, it turned out to be a guy named Lindsay. I sigh softly with relief, but it doesn't make the nauseous feeling go away.

Nathan paid for our entry, and we made our way to the gift shop. I look around for something to wear. I decided on a dark purple tankini with floral patterns. Nathan pays for it and tells me to go try it on. There was no mirror in the changing room, so I couldn't see how the swimsuit looked on me. All I know is that it made me feel naked. It wasn't something I was used to wearing.

Taking a deep breath, silently telling myself that I can do this, I step out of the changing room. Nathan is waiting for me. As soon as he sees me emerge, I wasn't sure if I should slap him or something. He scans his eyes up and down my body, immediately making me feel uncomfortable for wearing this. I shouldn't be wearing this. What was I thinking when I picked it out?

I try to cover myself with my arms.

"It looks stupid, doesn't it?" I say.

Nathan meets my eyes. "Stupid?" He shakes his head. "No. It doesn't look stupid. You look great in it, Alex."

I blush at his words.

Before I can decide that this is a stupid idea and change out of this suit, Nathan grabs my wrist, pulling me along with him. My heart races in my chest as we walk past people and went to the locker we hired to place our belongings inside.

"You realise how much I hate you for making me come here?" I tell him. I want to feel anger, but I can't feel it. It was as if Nathan had taken it away from me. Normally I wouldn't have agreed to be here with him. I could have hung up the phone, but I didn't. I let him lead me here. Because deep down inside I knew it had something to do with the conversation we had yesterday when he found me at the park. The way he listened to me as I spoke. I think it was having some kind of effect on me.

"Well, I don't see you doing anything to stop me." He winks his eyes at me and smiles.

The butterflies reappear in my stomach. I put my hand over it, still not fully understanding this feeling.

"Why did you bring me here in the first place?" I want to know.

"I told you. I thought it would be a great place for us to hang out and get to know each other."

"It's not even hot today." It was a warm day, not warm enough for me to want to go swimming.

"I know, but it's still warm."

"We agreed to do something on Monday night, not today," I reminded him. All I want to do right now is to be at home and draw. I need to draw. Maybe it was just the fear of being seen with Nathan, but I'd rather be at home where I can express how I feel through my artwork. I couldn't be here with Nathan. What will people say if they see me with him?

"I know that's what we agreed to do."

I frown at him. Why did this jerk bring me here? "Then why did you change the plans?"

He opens the locker and puts his bag inside. "Like I said, the plan on Monday I want to do doesn't leave us much time getting to know each other. So I thought this place was the perfect opportunity for us to get to know each other."

"Maybe I like the idea of us not getting to know each other." I want to go home where I can be alone.

Nathan gives me a cheeky smile. "Yeah, I don't think that's what you're going to say once we have fun."

I was going to tell him I don't like to have fun when he takes off his t-shirt, showing off his torso. He didn't seem like the guy who worked out, but I stopped breathing for a second as I stared at his perfect toned body. Nathan puts his shirt in the locker and grabs a bottle of sunscreen from his bag. He asks me if I would like some. I hold out my palm and he squirts the cream into it. I rub it onto my arms and face. Nathan does the same, and I can't help but watch as he rubs the cream onto his body.

Alex, stop this! I think to myself. *What are you doing? Nathan is the enemy here. You can't like him!*

"You're blushing."

I snap my eyes away from his chest and look up at him. "What? No, I'm not."

"Yes, you are. You look cute when you blush."

"Don't call me cute."

He chuckles. "Sorry. Come on, let's go."

He grabs my wrist, but I quickly push him away.

"Rule number one. Do not touch me unless I tell you to," I warn him.

He nods. "Okay. Come on. What slide would you like to go on?"

"None."

"How about I choose something and then you can pick the next one?"

I agree to allow him to pick the first slide. He decides the Tropical Cyclone, a cone shape slide that looked like a funnel from a tornado, is what we should go down first. I wasn't sure about the whole idea with it because I had to slide down with Nathan. The idea of having his body pressed up against me terrified me. I couldn't go down it with him. I want to go down the slide on my own, but I know he will want me to go with him. The next slide we go to, I will make sure you go down it yourself.

We stand in line to go up to the slide. It's long, and it feels like it isn't moving at all. This is why I don't go to places like this. What's the point of coming here if all you're going to do is stand all day in a line?

"Remind me to kill you later once you drop me at home," I say to Nathan. There are at least ten people in front of us now.

"Why is that?" he asks, turning to face me. He doesn't look scared at all over my threat. Why isn't he scared of me like others are?

"For making me come up here."

"But you're enjoying it, aren't you?"

"Not while I'm standing in this line."

"Yeah, I know. The lines are the worst, but I promise you once we get to the top, it will be fun."

Five minutes passed until it was finally our turn. Nathan sits down on the plastic float first, and I sit down in front of him. Nathan wraps his arms around my waist, his chest pressing up against my back. I drew a breath as his skin touches mine. With his body so close to me, my brain goes into panic mode. What am I doing? I shouldn't be this close to him.

I want to get out of here.

"You guys ready?" the slide operator asks us.

Nathan answers yes. I nod, afraid if I spoke, my voice would break. Why does it feel like I'm making a mistake for being here with him? I hang onto the float, preparing myself. The slide operator pushes us through the tunnel, and the water moves the float along.

"Hold on," Nathan tells me.

The float picks up speed the further we go down the tunnel, twisting the corners. Nathan screams with excitement, while I couldn't decide if I should scream or not. My brain screams at me to join in the fun with Nathan, but my body just didn't know how to respond to it.

We finally see the light at the end of the tunnel, landing in the pool. Nathan is still screaming, and it made me feel like a complete fool for not acting the way he is. I look around and see everyone around me having fun. In a nearby pool, I see a young girl with her father, splashing each other in the pool. Seeing them sends an ache to my heart at the memory of my father. Why couldn't I have fun like that father and daughter? Why was I so afraid to have fun?

Because you know it will bring back memories of him, my brain tells me.

"So, what do you think?" Nathan asks as we swim out of the pool.

"I don't know. I guess it was okay."

"You guess?" He arches an eyebrow. "You don't sound so convinced." He climbs out and then helps me out as well. "You meant to be jumping around with excitement. Please tell me you had fun going down the slide. All I could hear was my voice going down that tunnel."

"Maybe I'm not much of a screamer."

"So, what slide are we going on next?" he asks.

I look around, trying to think which one. I see a tower that is six stories high. There were different colour slides coming out in all directions. One catches my eye—a green and blue tube. It goes down and has a loop in the middle before leading the rest of the tube into the pool.

I point to it and tell Nathan I want to go on that one. He agrees to go, and we join the line leading up to it. We take a while to get up there, and when we do, we position ourselves on the tunnel. Nathan gets blue and I get green.

"See you at the bottom, Alex," he says, winking at me.

I narrow my eyes at him with a smile. "Beat me, and you're dead."

He pokes his tongue out at me.

The slide operator tells us to go. Tucking my arms down beside me, I slide down the tunnel. The water carries me down. I want to scream. No one is here to hear me scream. It feels as if half of me was telling me to have fun, and the other half is telling myself I couldn't. I can't have fun. Not without Dad. Nothing feels right with him.

The panicking starts just at the thought of having fun without Dad. My chest tightens, and I find it difficult to breathe, suddenly feeling claustrophobic inside this tunnel. I need to get out of here. I can't be here, and I most definitely couldn't be here with Nathan. Having fun is the last thing I should be having.

I hit the bottom of the water. Under the water, I couldn't breathe, as if all the air was gone. My lungs burn for air. I swim to the surface, but it feels like I still couldn't breathe.

"Yes! I won!" I hear Nathan say. He then swims over to me. "Alex, are you okay?"

The concern in his voice helps me to take a couple of deep breaths. *Breathe, Alex, breathe.*

"I want to go home," I say once I get my breath back.

Nathan looks at me, unsure if I was serious or not. "Alex, come on. We are just having fun."

"I said, take me home!" I say through my teeth.

He nods, saying nothing, probably afraid to say something in case I snap at him or make a scene. We get out of the pool and walk to our locker, grabbing our stuff. I storm off to the changing room and hide into a stall, stripping off my swimsuit and stare at it on the floor. I stand there naked, shivering, fighting to hold the tears back. They flow out so swiftly. I wipe them before someone hears me sobbing and knocks on the door to see if I was okay, changing back into my clothes.

I step out of the changing room where Nathan waits for me.

"Alex, if I upset you, I'm sorry," he says quickly. "We don't need to leave."

I bite my lip. Why can't I tell him what's really upsetting me rather than letting him take the blame for my sudden outburst?

He cautiously steps towards me. "Alex, please tell me what's wrong."

"I want to go home, Nathan. Don't ask me anymore questions. Just take me home."

He nods. "Okay."

We head back to the car in silence. Neither of us said a word to each other on the way home.

Nathan drops me off at the park. He says goodbye, but I say nothing in return, not even a thank you or see you later. I watch him drive away until I could no longer see his car.

I head home. As I near my house, I see Dereck's car parked on the street. I frown at it. What is that jerk doing here again?

I head inside, walking through the house to the backyard. Mum and Dereck are in the kitchen, eating a sandwich.

Mum smiles, greeting me. "How was the park?"

"Fine," I answer.

"Did you go swimming?" She eyes the swimsuit in my hand. "Where did you go swimming?"

Stop talking, Mum, I wanted to say, afraid she will expose my lies to where I really was.

"Nowhere," I answer.

I could see Mum wanted to press more questions about my whereabouts, but with Dereck here, she didn't want to cause another argument with me. So instead she asks me, "Would you like a sandwich? I can make you one."

I look between her and Dereck. No way was I sitting down at the table with them. Without answering Mum, I walk outside. Mum keeps the pegs in a bucket beside the clothesline. I hung up the swimsuit and headed back inside. Mum tries to get me to talk, asking me if everything is okay, but I ran out of the kitchen before she saw the tears in my eyes.

Once locked in my room, I lie down on my bed and cry.

Why Dad? Why did you leave me like this? Don't you see the pain it is causing me?

Chapter 15

I spent most of my weekend in my room. It was best for everyone that I did. After the announcement of the engagement and what happened at Splash Resort, I just didn't want to talk to anyone. Nathan tries calling a few times, but I only ignore him. He was the one person I didn't want to talk to. I know he needed some kind of explanation for what happened, but right now I don't want to tell him anything. He wouldn't understand.

Maybe I could avoid everyone over the weekend, but of course when Monday rolls around, I couldn't avoid Nathan. The first thing he will do is ask me what happened on Saturday. I haven't even prepared for what I wanted to tell him.

I sit outside the library, concentrating on my latest drawing before roll call.

I spotted Nathan approaching me from the corner of my eye. I pretend I don't see him and stare at my drawing, as if I were trying to figure out what I wanted to draw even though I already knew. Maybe if I keep my eyes down, he won't notice me and he will keep walking along.

But of course that was wishful thinking. He has already noticed me.

He stands in front of me. I don't dare look up, like maybe he will get the message that I don't want to talk to him after what happened on Saturday, and he will walk away, forgetting the whole thing. But this was Nathan Bridges. He wasn't afraid of me. He will do whatever it takes to get me to talk. Nathan is here for an explanation as to why I had a panic attack at the water park and demanded he took me home.

The thing is, I don't know why I had the panic attack. It's the first time it has happened.

"Are you interested in seeing Hurricane live tonight?" Nathan asks me.

I look up at him, my eyes darting to the digital ticket on his phone. Asking me to go to a concert with him tonight it not what I expected. Wasn't he going to ask me about Saturday? I force myself to look at Nathan. His eyes pleaded with me to say yes. Is he crazy for talking to me right here? I thought I told him not to talk to me here. What if people hear our conversation?

I glance around, making sure no one from our grade was nearby. No one looks our way as they walk on by with friends and chat about their weekend. I turn back to him. "Are you seriously taking me to a Hurricane concert?"

Hurricane is a Canadian pop-punk band that is touring our country at the moment. They have a show here in Sydney tonight. I sometimes listen to their music. Compared to many of the bands I listen to, Hurricane always has this comforting feel about their music that always makes me feel better.

But even if they're a great band, I wasn't interested in seeing them live. Concerts weren't for me. I can't believe Nathan is actually taking me to a concert for our first date. Don't people normally go on dates to a restaurant or a movie? Who on earth goes to a concert on their first date?

What if I agree to go to this concert, and I have another panic attack?

"Look, I know a concert is not exactly an ideal place to go on a date," Nathan tells me. "Especially for a first date. But I really want to see them live. My older brother was supposed to go with me until he bailed a couple of days ago. I would ask Eric, but he has something on tonight."

I sigh. I don't exactly have a choice here, so I might as well say yes. Even if I say no, he will take me somewhere else I don't want to be. "Okay, fine. I will go. Now get out of here before someone sees you talking to me."

Nathan promises to pick me up around four thirty. The concert starts at six o'clock.

He turns to leave, but then stops short, turning back to me. "Just one more thing before I leave you alone."

I sigh. Why can't he just leave me alone already? "What?"

"I want to know what happened on Saturday. Why did you suddenly freak out? Did I upset you?"

And there's the question he wanted to know that I knew I couldn't avoid forever. How do I tell him what happened when I wasn't sure myself? This was the first panic attack I've experienced.

"I don't know," I bluntly tell him. It's all I could say until I can figure out what is wrong with me. "I just did. Now go before someone sees us."

Nathan stares at me, nods slowly, like he is trying to figure me out. Without a word, he leaves. I watch him as he heads inside the building. Once he is gone, I look around me. There's no one I knew watching. Not even the people walking past took notice of us talking. Good. We are safe.

I sit there for a moment, thinking about tonight and how the concert will be. I could enjoy it, shouldn't I? What if I were to have another panic attack again?

"So, what were you and Nathan talking about?"

I jump at the sound of my sister's voice, snapping me out of my thoughts. I turn to her, clutching my sketchbook to my chest. "It's none of your business."

I stand up and push my sister out of the way. I headed in the opposite direction Nathan had. Lindsay follows me. I roll my eyes. Does she really have to follow me right now? Why can't she just leave me alone for once in her life?

"Alex, you have to help me get Nathan to like me. He is way too obsessed with you to notice me."

Seriously? Is that why she is bothering me, hoping I could help her get Nathan to notice her? Why does she even want him? Can't she see he isn't interested? Lindsay has a boyfriend. What's wrong with him for her to go after Nathan?

"Lindsay," I firmly say, "I'm not doing your dirty work for you. Why are you chasing after him, anyway? You have a boyfriend."

Lindsay rolls her eyes. "So? What is it to you? Yes, I know I have one, but I also told you before that I'm experimenting with different guys, okay?"

I raise an eyebrow. "Really? By cheating on Simon? Imagine how he will feel when he finds out you're seeing other guys behind his back."

"Look, I love Simon, okay? It's just sometimes I'm not sure if we're meant to be. I want us to still be together, but I want to explore my options. Maybe I will find someone I really want to be with. He doesn't know I'm cheating on him, and I would prefer if he didn't know."

As much as I hate Simon, I would hate to be him when he finds out what my sister is doing to him.

"Why don't you break up with him, Lindsay? What you are doing is wrong. To be in a relationship, you should be with one person only, not sleeping around with others. Imagine how Simon will feel once he finds out how unfaithful you have been to him."

"Can we forget about me for a second? Let's focus on you. Do you like Nathan?"

Her question is so out of the blue. I can't answer her because I know whatever she asked me is stupid. Yeah, whatever. Nathan has a crush on me. It doesn't mean I like him in return. And it definitely does not mean that because we hung out on Saturday that I like him either. I don't.

I sigh and turn away as I head inside the building. I don't need to tell her anything. She should already know the answer.

I hate Nathan Bridges, and I will never like him.

Lindsay follows me. "Hello? Earth to Alex. Are you going to answer me? Do you like Nathan?"

I stop near the stairs and turn to my sister. "Do you have somewhere to be, Lindsay?"

Lindsay shakes her head. "No. I don't have to be anywhere. Just give me an answer, Alex."

I roll my eyes. She really doesn't know how to give up, does she? "Why would I like Nathan?" I walk up the stairs. "He is nothing but an annoying jerk who won't leave me alone."

Lindsay follows me up the stairs. "Why can't you give me a simple, straight answer?"

The bell rings, saving me from answering my sister. People head into the building to head towards their roll call. I quickly hurry off to mine before Lindsay could ask me something else. I know I can't run away from her completely because we are in the same roll call together. She will hassle me there until I answer her.

I sit down in the classroom and open my sketchbook. Before I could put pencil to paper, Lindsay came up to me. I quickly close it before she sees it.

"Alex, why can't you answer my question? What's so hard about answering it? You do this all the time whenever I ask you something."

"How many times do I have to tell you to leave me alone and keep out of my private life?"

"I don't care about your private life, Alex. I just want to know the answer."

"There is no answer, Lindsay. I don't like him, okay?"

Lindsay is about to open her mouth to answer when Mr Grey walks into the room to mark the roll. He asks my sister to take a seat. We stare at each other for a moment. She stares at me like she is trying to figure me out. Like maybe if she did, she would have the answer to every secret I have. She will never figure it out. I won't let her. We may have been able to read each other's minds when we were younger. Now that we have drifted apart, we hardly know what the other is thinking.

She listens to our teacher and takes a seat at the front of the room. As Mr Grey speaks, I open up my book to sketch as the rest of the class settles down to have their names marked off.

***

So many things are running through my head that I'm still trying to make sense of. Especially with everything that happened on Saturday with the butterflies and the panic attack. The only person I could speak to about this is Miss Giovanni. I make my way to her office at recess. She will know what is wrong with me. Even if I don't enjoy talking to people about anything, she always tells me to talk about anything to her that might bother me.

But when I'm sitting in her office, I can't think of how to tell her anything. My brain freezes up. Like it was afraid to know the answer to my panic attack. Or maybe I was just afraid to discover something new about myself.

"Alex, are you sure you want to tell me what's bothering you now?" Miss Giovanni asks me when I don't speak for the last ten minutes. "Maybe you would like to tell me another day."

I fiddle with my sketchbook on my lap. I shake my head. *Come on, Alex. You can speak.* "No. I want to tell you."

"Then tell me," she says with a friendly smile. "You have been sitting here for at least ten minutes, staring down at your lap. Tell me, Alex. What's on your mind?"

I take a breath. I can trust Miss Giovanni. Everything I tell her is confidential. Why am I so afraid to tell her, as if someone will find out?

"Something happened on Saturday," I say.

She opens her notebook and writes something down. I hate it when she writes things down. It makes me nervous wondering what she could write about. She doesn't always take notes, but when she does, I wonder if they are good or bad.

"What happened, Alex?" she asks, encouraging me to continue on.

I tell her about Nathan, Splash Resort, and the panic attack.

The only thing I don't tell her about is the butterflies I felt around Nathan that day. She doesn't need to know about that. I'm sure they meant nothing. I don't like Nathan.

"Have you ever experienced a panic attack before, Alex?" Miss Giovanni asks me.

I shake my head. "No, it was my first time. I didn't want to go with him in the first place, but he insisted I come along. He thought coming to the park would be good for me. I don't even know how I allowed him to talk me into coming along with him. He was kind enough to pay my entry and to buy me a swimsuit. The first slide I went on with him, I felt nauseous. When we went on the second one, I had a panic attack."

"What do you think might have triggered the attack?"

I shrug. "I don't know. Maybe seeing kids with their fathers brought back memories of my dad. And then, when I was going down the slide, the thought of having fun terrified me. Like it was wrong for me to have fun without my dad. That's when I panicked."

"Why do you think it's wrong to have fun without your dad?"

Why do I think it's wrong to have fun without Dad?

"I don't know," I say. "When Dad left, I felt lost. Having fun just never felt right without him."

"There's nothing wrong with you having fun, Alex. Your dad leaving should have nothing to do with you not having fun. I understand losing him must have been hard for you. But remember that life goes on, and you shouldn't have someone hold you back from living your life. If you want to go have fun, go out and have fun, Alex. Don't let nothing or anyone stop you."

I sit there for a moment to think about what she had said. I know she's right, but still I wasn't sure how I was supposed to have fun without thinking about memories of dad.

"When was the last time you had fun, Alex?" Miss Giovanni asks me.

I shrug. When was the last time I had fun? I have a brief memory of planning Lindsay's and my twelfth birthday with Dad, telling him all the things we wanted for our party the week before he left. It was just a simple party in our backyard with friends and family. Anything after that week, I can't remember. It's all just a blur. After all, it has been six years since Dad left. When he left, it felt as if I couldn't have fun. Not without him. If I even tried to have any kind of fun, it left me feeling guilty because Dad wasn't there with me to share in the excitement.

I mentioned this to Miss Giovanni.

"So you feel you can't have fun without your dad?" she asks me.

I nod. "It makes me feel bad, like I'm going to get into trouble with him or something."

"What about anything else? How do you feel about other things? Like with Nathan when he asked you to go with him, how did you feel?"

"I didn't want to go. Lindsay said he has a crush on me. He asked me out, but I said no. He then asked if I wanted to go just as friends."

"And what happened when you went with him? Did you feel you could be friends? I know you said you don't want any friends."

"It feels weird since I haven't had a friend for so many years. I don't know what he sees in me."

"Have you ever had a friend who was a guy before?"

I shake my head. "No."

"How do you feel about having Nathan as a friend? Do you want to be his friend after the time you spent with him this weekend?"

I chew my bottom lip, thinking about him and how I kept having this weird feeling in the pit of my stomach whenever he was around. "I don't know how I feel about Nathan, let alone to be friends. What if I make a friend, get really close to them, and they suddenly leave me? I don't know if I can take another person leaving me again after Dad left me."

"Is that what you think Nathan will do? Leave you?"

"It's possible he could."

"Describe to me how you felt when your dad left you."

Tears prick my eyes. I couldn't think about Dad. Not right now. I don't want to think of the day he left me. My twelfth birthday is the only thing I never want to remember for as long as I live. It's too painful for me to think about. The pain of thinking that someone you cared about doesn't love you enough to stay with you. Out of all the days Dad could have left, why did he choose my birthday?

"I'm sorry. I need to go, Miss Giovanni," I say, getting up. "The bell will ring soon."

"Alex, you can stay."

"No. I should get to class."

I walk over to the door.

"Alex, wait. Before you go, I have something for you."
She takes something out of her top drawer. It's a purple
spiral notebook. She gets off her chair and walks over to
me. "I was thinking of you over the weekend. Now, I know
you like to draw and that relaxes you, but I feel that you
have a lot of anger stuck inside of you. Drawing is good,
but writing is also good. I got you this notebook. I thought
maybe you can use it to write how you feel down."

I take the notebook, staring at it. Why would I need a
notebook for? I don't need to write my emotions down. I
can express how I feel in my sketchbook.

Thanking her, I leave the office and slip the notebook
into my bag. I doubt I will need it, but I will keep it in
my bag. Hopefully the next time I see Miss Giovanni, she
doesn't ask me if I have written in it.

Chapter 16

I stare at my reflection in the mirror. Were jeans and a long sleeve stripe shirt good enough to wear on a date or to a pop-punk concert? It was a cool night for February, but it will probably be humid inside the concert hall. My hair hangs loose around my shoulders. I experiment with my hair, trying to decide if I should have it in or out. I don't know why it bothered me to look good for Nathan. It's not like I was trying to impress him.

To finish my look, I tied my hair into a ponytail. Taking one last look in the mirror, I grab a small bag to put my wallet inside and sling it over my shoulder, heading downstairs. I sneak past my sister's room. I don't want her to know anything about my date with Nathan tonight. She will ask all kinds of questions. Mum got off work early today, and was in the kitchen preparing dinner. The good thing is Dereck isn't here tonight.

"Mum, I'm going out to a concert," I tell her.

Mum looks up from where she was cutting carrots. The expression she gave me showed she wasn't sure if I was joshing or not. "A concert? That's exciting. Is Lindsay going too?"

I shake my head. "No."

She smiles. "What concert are you going to?"

"I'm seeing Hurricane."

"Are you going on your own? I wasn't aware of you purchasing tickets for a concert. You could have told me earlier, Alex."

I bite my lip. Why do I feel shy about talking to her about Nathan? I could tell her about him, but I didn't want her to think something was going on between Nathan and me.

"I'm sorry it is last minute. I'm going with a friend. They only invited me to the concert today."

Mum smiles. "Is this friend of yours name Nathan?"

I blush. "Maybe."

"Well, okay. But next time inform me earlier about your plans. You have a good time, Alex. Come straight home after the concert. You have school tomorrow."

I nod and then walk out the door.

I wait outside on the kerb for Nathan. He pulls up within a few minutes, showing up at exactly 4:30 like he'd promised. He was going to get out and open the door for me, but I'm already opening the passenger side door for myself and climbing into the vehicle.

Nathan greets me, and I return the greeting. I take in his jeans and Hurricane t-shirt. My heart does a flip when I notice how great he looked in black.

Alex, focus, I remind myself. *You're supposed to hate Nathan. Do not take notice of how great he looks in a certain colour.*

"All set?" he asks me as I put on my seat belt.

I nod and he sets off down the street.

"You look nice," he says, keeping his eyes ahead like he was afraid to look at me as he said it.

My heart does a flip at his compliment. Why is it doing that?

"Thank you," I answer.

As Nathan drives, he tries to make small talk with me. I wasn't up for talking, unsure what to say to him, but I forced myself to answer back. I keep my eyes ahead through the entire drive, afraid my heart will do more flips, or that maybe butterflies will appear next. If I were getting these strange feelings, what would it be like for the rest of the night?

***

Nathan shows the usher our tickets, and we entered the building. Nathan leads me to the front of the stage where a small crowd was already forming, while another crowd gathered at the merchandise booth. We got a spot right in the front row, standing behind the barrier that separated the audience from the stage. I watch the people around me as teens and early twenty-something-year-olds were talking about the band to each other. I feel a little left out, not knowing a thing about the band. Sure, I hear their music occasionally on the radio, but I don't listen to them much. But when their music comes onto the radio, it always gives me a comforting feeling more than other music I listen to.

"Have you ever been to a concert before?" Nathan asks me. "Or is this your first one?"

Here we go again. The small talk that I want to avoid so much.

"This is my first concert," I say.

Nathan smiles. "Well, I'm honoured to take you to your first concert. You're going to love Hurricane. I saw them once a couple of years ago when they first came out to Australia."

I feel nausea when he said I will love the concert.

What happens if I have another panic attack if I enjoy myself?

"What if I don't like their music?" I ask. It's only half a lie because I mainly hear their songs that are played on the radio. I do not know what their other music is like. Will I get the same comforting feel with their other songs, like the ones I hear on the radio?

Nathan shakes his head. "You won't hate their music. I swear you're going to love them. This concert will be something you will always remember for your first.

Hurricane is one of my favourite bands. Their music always makes me feel better, like I am not alone."

My heart skips a beat knowing that Nathan felt the same way as I did when I listen to Hurricane's music.

Within half an hour, Hurricane fans filled the theatre. Another half an hour passed, and the opening band came on. My ears hurt from the screaming made by the surrounding fans. All I wanted was to tell them to shut up, but I couldn't do that. I will ruin this for Nathan. I don't care if he hates me or not, but I know I couldn't ruin this night for him. Behind me, some girls pushed me forward. I stumble. Thankfully, the barrier was in front of me. Why do people say that concerts are fun if people push you around?

I was about to turn around to give the girls a piece of my mind when Nathan stopped me.

He puts his hands on my shoulder. "Don't, Alex. They aren't worth saying anything to. They will only make it worse for you."

"They won't stop pushing."

"I know. Some people just don't care because tonight it's about them, not you or anyone else. The shoving will get worse once Hurricane comes onto the stage because everyone is going to want to get closer to them. Promise me you won't say anything to them?"

I nod, even though I wasn't sure how much longer I could hold my temper. "I promise."

He smiles. For a moment Nathan and I stood there staring at each other, forgetting about everyone around us and the opening band on the stage.

And then it happens. Butterflies appear in my stomach. A thousand thoughts were running through my head. My chest feels tight, and I was sure another panic attack was going to happen. I don't understand this feeling Nathan is making me feel.

In my mind, I imagine Nathan leaning closer to me and brushing his lips against mine. And for a moment, I thought that's exactly what he was going to do, but he didn't.

Luckily, the lights were low, and Nathan couldn't see me blushing.

I was glad when Nathan broke eye contact with me, turning his attention to the band on the stage. I stand there, staring at a spot on the floor, unable to look up at the stage, afraid of what would happen if I laid my eyes on Nathan again.

When the opening band finishes their set, I knew the next half hour would be torture being alone with Nathan. Not with the small talk, but with the strange feeling I'm getting around him. He asked me how I liked the opening band. I answered they were okay, though it wasn't my taste in music. The butterflies danced around my stomach as we speak. Why can't these stupid butterflies go away?

Whatever I'm feeling, I shouldn't be feeling this way towards Nathan.

Hurricane soon comes onto the stage. Music plays as the lights dim on the stage, and the five members move around the stage to position themselves. The band opens with one of their songs I don't recognise. The stage lights come back on, revealing the members. Fans around me began screaming like crazy, jumping up and down with excitement at their idols. Nathan wasn't screaming, but he cheered with excitement. Right then and now I felt like an outcast, as I was the only one who wasn't excited to see this band live.

The music is so loud that I can't even hear myself think. I feel a headache coming on. The lead singer, Jason, encourages the audience to sing along with him. I glance over at Nathan. He is singing along. I may have heard several songs by Hurricane, but I don't know them well enough to know the lyrics off by heart. Amongst this crowd, I was surely the odd one out for not knowing the lyrics. I feel stupid. I shouldn't have said yes to Nathan. If I hadn't agreed to come, I would be at home right now, fighting with Lindsay. Or maybe I would have locked myself in my room, drawing.

But it feels good to get out of the house. It felt good to be here with Nathan.

The band ends their first song. Jason gives a short greeting to the audience and then goes straight into the next song. My body wants to dance to the music, but I reminded myself that I hated dancing. My mind was also telling me I couldn't have fun, or I will have another panic attack. I couldn't have one here.

I glance over at Nathan. He is fully into the music, happily singing along. Why can't I do the same?

He catches me staring at him and turns to me, smiling. It was like his smile was contagious, and I couldn't help but return one.

"Sing along," Nathan shouts to be heard over the music.

I shake my head. "I can't."

"Why not?"

"I don't know the lyrics." This was part true, but I couldn't tell Nathan the real reason I didn't want to sing. He wouldn't understand why I experience panic attacks when I try to have fun. It may have happened only once, so I didn't know if what Miss Giovanni had told me earlier was true, but I didn't want to go through it again. Not here in front of everyone. I didn't want to ruin this night for Nathan.

"So?" he smiles. "It doesn't matter, Alex. No one cares if you don't know the lyrics. No one can hear you anyway. Come on, sing."

I stumble along with the lyrics. I say them quietly, afraid someone was going to hear me, but Nathan is right. No one can hear me over the music. Their focus is on the band.

I feel someone's hand slipping into mine. I panic, ready to punch the person near me for touching me, when I realise it was just Nathan. He smiles brightly at me, and I return a shy smile. He squeezes my hand, as to say that everything was going to be okay.

I can do this. Everything is going to be alright.

***

I made it through the concert without experiencing a panic attack. By the time it ended, I didn't want it to end. Even when my head hurts from all the loud music and screaming fans. I wanted more of the music. Nathan was right. The music from this band made you feel like you weren't alone; all my anxiety with the panic attack was gone, like I never thought about it.

For most of our ride home, Nathan and I sat there in silence. We talked a bit about the concert, but I wasn't really in the mood for talking. I just wanted to rest my head. I should have brought something for my headache with me.

"Thanks for taking me out tonight," I say to Nathan as we enter Wakefield, getting closer to home. "I had a good time."

Nathan turns to me, his eyes widening when I mentioned I had a good time. "You actually had fun?" He turns his eyes back to the road.

"Yeah." I give him a small smile. I can't believe I'm admitting this to myself. It reminded me of the good times I used to have with my family and friends before Dad walked out on us. Why did I let him stop me from having fun? "I have had much fun in a real long time. Hurricane put on a great show. I really enjoyed it."

And I really miss having fun, I add silently to myself.

"How come you don't like having fun?" Nathan wants to know.

I don't answer him. I can't tell him the things I told Miss Giovanni. Not yet.

I stare out of the window at the houses that we pass by. We are getting closer to my street, just four blocks more.

"Alex?" Nathan calls me when I didn't answer him after a long silence.

Do I really want to tell him what happened to Dad? What if I tell him, and he doesn't want to be friends with me anymore? What if I get close to him, and then he disappears?

"When I'm ready," I answer him, still staring out of the window, unable to look at him, "I will tell you the reason. At the moment I don't want anyone to know why I hate everyone and everything."

I can feel Nathan's eyes on me, but I feel afraid to turn to look at him.

"That's fine, Alex.," he says. "Take your time. Tell me when you are ready. So, since you had a good time tonight, do you want to go out again?"

This time I turn away from the window, turning to face Nathan. Half of me wanted to go out with him, the other half didn't want to. "I will think about it."

Chapter 17

For the first time, I was actually excited about attending German. I take my usual spot in the back beside the window. Nathan takes a seat a couple of rows down from me where he sits with Eric. He looks my way and smiles. Butterflies dance around my stomach as I return the smile.

Mr Brown takes his position at the front of the class and begins the lesson. Rather than paying attention to him, I sketch in my book. I sneak glances at Nathan, making sure no one sees me, and sketch Nathan carefully from the side of his face. He concentrates hard on Mr Brown as he speaks. As I outlined Nathan, it felt weird to be drawing someone else other than my dad all the time.

As soon as class is over, I race out of the classroom before Nathan could talk to me. I didn't want to be caught chatting to him or have anyone suspect something is going on between us. I make my way to the library where I can spend recess. Finding a seat at a table in the back corner, I sit down and pull out my sketchbook, continuing with my drawing from class.

"Where were you last night?" I hear my sister's voice from behind me.

I swiftly snap my book closed and turn to see my sister walking over to me, frowning. She stops beside me and crosses her arms across her chest.

"Why do you care where I was?" I ask.

"Why do I care?" Lindsay unfolds her arms and places her hands on her hips. "I care because I find it strange that my sister, who *hates everything*, went out when she never goes out. So where were you last night?"

I sigh. Does Lindsay really have to do this right now when all I want to be is alone?

"I went nowhere, Lindsay." There is no way I'm telling her about the concert. If I do, she will want to know who I went with. And if she finds out I went with Nathan, she will ask all kinds of questions I don't want to answer.

"Bull crap, Alex. You were out with Nathan last night, weren't you?"

My heart pounds in my chest. She knows. Oh God, she knows I went out with him. I should be able to open up to my sister and tell her all about the date I went on with Nathan, but I couldn't. I couldn't tell her the truth about anything. Lindsay will make fun of me for being with him. She will probably be jealous since she is the one who fancies him. She will accuse me of stealing him, which I am not.

I scoff. "Why would I go out with Nathan? I rather die than go out with that jerk."

Lindsay stares at me hard, like she was trying to see into my soul. She knows I'm lying. It's our twin thing that we do. We know whenever one of us is lying. As kids growing up, we could hide nothing from each other without knowing the truth. If someone else were to ask me if I was out with Nathan, they would believe my lies. They will end the discussion before they get their head torn off by me. Lindsay will keep pestering me with questions until I finally crack and tell her the truth.

"You like him," she answers for me. "That's why you would go out with Nathan."

I freeze, my heart beating fast in my chest. It causes nausea to rise.

She knows.

Wait. No. I don't like him. Lindsay doesn't know what she is talking about. I don't like Nathan. I never had and I never will. We are just friends... I think that's what we are. I don't know if I even want to be friends with him. Just because we hung out at Splash Resort and attended the Hurricane concert, it doesn't mean anything is going on between us.

I needed to think fast so my sister doesn't get suspicious. I needed to act like myself or she will definitely know something is up.

I roll my eyes. "That would be the day. Look, Lindsay, I never went out with Nathan. Why would I even go out with that jerk? I don't like him."

Liar! My brain screams at me.

My head spins. These questions, feared of being caught in a lie and triggering my fears, were too overwhelming.

"Girls, could you please keep it down in here," the librarian warns us. "If you don't, I will have to ask you to leave."

"Alex, there's nothing wrong with admitting how you feel towards someone," Lindsay continues, completely ignoring whatever the librarian had said. "Why can't you at least tell me you're crushing on Nathan? We used to tell each other everything."

"I don't need to admit anything to you."

I stand up quickly, and I really wish I hadn't. I feel lightheaded. Lindsay sees that something is wrong. She is asking me if I'm okay, but I don't answer her. I need to get out of here. I need to clear my head.

I turn to grab my stuff before collapsing onto the floor.

***

I wake up in the sick bay, alone, completely puzzled about my whereabouts. I grab my water bottle from my bag and take a sip before glancing at my watch. It's halfway through the third period. There is no reason to go back to class right now. I just have to wait here until the bell rings.

"You're awake." I look up to see the school nurse walking in. "How are you feeling?"

"What happened?" I ask, completely ignoring her question.

"You fainted in the library. Are you alright?"

I remember now. My panic attack caused me to be lightheaded when my sister tried to confront me about Nathan. Her questions and my lies overwhelmed me, and I feared she would find me out.

I nod. "Yeah, I'm alright."

"Have you eaten today? Do you have any food on you? If not, I can quickly duck down to the canteen to get you something."

I give her a small smile. "Thanks, but I'm alright. I have already eaten recess."

The nurse returns a smile. "That's good. Make sure you drink plenty of water. Just sit and relax in here until fourth period, and you can go to class. If you still feel lightheaded, I can call your mother."

I didn't want her to bother Mum. There was no reason to.

"I should be alright," I say. "Thank you."

The nurse leaves the room.

I pick up my sketchbook that's on the floor beside my bag. I opened it and turned to the page that I had been drawing. The side of Nathan's face stares back at me. The butterflies return as I picture his smiling face. No. What's happening to me? Why am I getting these butterflies? The nauseous feeling returns in the pit of my stomach. Is that lovesickness? Is that why I feel sick? I shouldn't be feeling this. I'm supposed to hate Nathan. Not get butterflies whenever I think about him.

I grab my stuff and go to see if Miss Giovanni is available. I need to see her. Only she can help me. I knock on her door and open it. She is with another student. She tells me to wait outside her office and will be with me soon. I only have to wait for another fifteen minutes before I can go in.

"I really need to talk to you about something, Miss Giovanni." I tell her, my voice panicking as I walk into her office.

"Calm down, Alex. Take a couple of deep breaths and take a seat," she tells me.

I listen, taking a few deep breaths and take a seat in front of her desk. She closes the door behind us and takes a seat opposite me.

When I have calmed down, Miss Giovanni smiles. "Tell me what's bothering you, Alex."

I open my mouth, but then I close it. Can I trust her with this? Of course I can. I just need to be open with her about it. She wouldn't judge me.

"I don't know what's wrong with me," I tell her. "Every time I think about Nathan or when I'm with him, I feel butterflies. Sometimes I feel nauseous, like I'm lovesick or something. Lindsay asked me if I liked him during recess today. It was like my head started spinning as I panicked about being caught liking him. I was told I fainted in the library."

"Yes, I heard you had fainted." She gives me a concerned smile. "Are you okay now?"

I nod, chewing my bottom lip. Was I really okay? "I think so. I don't really know. At the moment I'm just scared and confused."

"What are you scared and confused about?"

His name is on the tip of my tongue. Was I ready to admit this? "Nathan Bridges."

"Why do you feel scared and confused about him?"

My heart beat picks up again. I can tell her this. I can. She won't judge me.

"I think I might like him."

She smiles. "That's great, Alex. I'm happy for you."

I stare at her, puzzled. "How can you be happy for me or think that this is great? I don't want to like anyone. I'm supposed to *hate* everyone. When Lindsay questioned me, I wasn't sure what to tell her. I figured she would judge me for liking someone."

"Alex, no one is going to judge you. It's all in your head. You have built this wall around you after your dad left, that the idea of falling in love scares you because of what your dad did. You're trying to protect yourself from becoming hurt again. So hating everyone stops you from being hurt. You can't get hurt if you dislike everyone."

True, I can't get hurt by disliking everyone. From the moment I realised Dad wasn't returning, it felt like my entire world ended. I thought what if Mum left next? Or Lindsay? What will I do without them if they left too? Hating them and everyone else was one way I didn't have to get hurt if they left. And hating on everything so I didn't have to spend time with anyone. I also decided I will never fall in love. I didn't want to end up like my mother. Heartbroken by the person she thought loved her in return. I will not let myself get hurt.

But that was until I started liking Nathan.

I shouldn't like him. He's going to be like Dad and leave. I just know he will. I can't deal with that heartache again.

"Hating everyone is better than being hurt," I tell Miss Giovanni.

I wait for Miss Giovanni to say I'm being ridiculous, like what my sister would say. Instead, she says, "Love is a normal human emotion. We all feel it. And even if it means we will get hurt, it's part of life. No one wants to be hated, Alex. Including you."

The day Dad turned my world upside down and tore my family apart comes to my mind. How can one person do that without caring how the rest of us will feel?

"I'm afraid of what could happen again if I get close to someone like my dad if they leave," I say. "I don't remember the last time I ever felt love. When I'm around Nathan, I keep telling myself that I can't like him. I'm so terrified that if I let myself like him, I'm going to end up like my mother. I don't want to go through the pain she has gone through."

Miss Giovanni gives me an assuring smile. "Alex, I know you're scared. We all have someone we are close to leave us. Yes, it's going to hurt, but we can't let one bad experience stop us from caring about others."

I nod, looking down at my sketchbook. I knew she was right, but I wanted to feel I'm doing the right thing, that I didn't need anyone in my life to care about.

"How long have you felt this way towards Nathan?" Miss Giovanni wants to know.

I thought of my time with Nathan at the concert. The way his hand fitted perfectly in mine, and the way his smile gave me butterflies.

I force myself to look up at my counsellor. "Yesterday."

She nods. She jots something down in her notes before looking up at me. "Alex, do you experience panic attacks around Nathan?"

I shake my head. "No. Just a feeling of nausea and butterflies. My heart races and it scares me."

Miss Giovanni smiles. "It's just a normal reaction when you have a crush on somebody. You have no reason to be scared, Alex. It's up to you, but you could always tell Nathan how you feel. He likes you too, doesn't he?"

I nod. "He does."

"Then you should tell him how you feel, Alex. See how things go with him. It will be good for you to explore this emotion. It could help you have a whole new outlook on everything."

I clutch my sketchbook closer to me. I couldn't quite make eye contact with Miss Giovanni. A whole new outlook on everything. Is that something I wanted? What if things didn't work out the way they did? What if I'm left heartbroken?

Miss Giovanni gives me an assuring smile. "Alex, there is no reason for you to feel scared. Of course, it's normal to feel scared of these new feelings when you first have a crush. But that fear doesn't hang around for long."

I sit there, unsure how I'm supposed to respond. What should I say? Should I say something else about Nathan?

When I say nothing, Miss Giovanni gestures towards my sketchbook. "Can I see your book, please?"

I hold on to my book, hesitating for a moment to give it to her. What is she going to say about my recent drawing? I don't even know why I drew it. I was just drawing how I felt that moment when I saw Nathan.

I hand the book over to her. She flips through it. I place my hands under my thighs to stop them from shaking, and bite down on my lip. A nauseous feeling appears in the pit of my stomach as I watch her get closer to my drawing of Nathan.

Miss Giovanni stops at a page and stares at it for a long time. My stomach drops. She sees the drawing.

She flips the book over in my direction and points to the picture of Nathan I had stretch earlier today in class, his face concentrating hard on what Mr Brown was talking about. "Is this Nathan?"

I nod, chewing my bottom lip. "Yes, it is."

She smiles, closing the book and hands it back to me. "It's good to see you drawing something else. Have you two gone out on a date?"

I smile, thinking about the other night and over the weekend. "We went to Splash Resort on Saturday. I don't know if that classifies as a date, but he wanted to go as friends. Last night he took me to see a concert."

"What concert did you see?"

"A band called Hurricane."

"How did the concert go?"

"It was good. I really enjoyed myself there."

"Did you have a panic attack?"

"I had a minor attack, but it was nothing like the one I had when we went to Splash Resort. I was terrified of having fun, but Nathan somehow helped me to overcome my fear. We had this moment just before the concert where I was sure we might kiss. I panicked inside, but I didn't show it."

"I'm thrilled for you, Alex. I like this new you, and I hope you continue this. Are you going to go out with him again?"

I shrug, smiling. "I don't know. We haven't decided yet, but I think we might."

The bell rings for fourth period. This was my chance to leave now that I have gotten out what I wanted to say. I thank Miss Giovanni for listening. When I didn't want to continue our conversation, she dismissed me. I left her office with a smile on my face.

The new Alex Jennings is what Miss Giovanni had said. Who is this new Alex Jennings? I wasn't sure. The thought of exploring new emotions terrified me, but I was glad I could explore them with Nathan. Whatever he sees in me, he sees something good that no one else can.

And maybe giving Nathan a chance will help me let go of whatever anger I feel towards my dad for leaving.

Chapter 18

I spent the afternoon in my room, sketching another picture of Nathan. This time it was a picture of him sitting with Eric under the shelter area. I sat near them at lunch, making sure Nathan didn't see me watching him as I drew.

Ever since I confessed to Miss Giovanni about how I felt towards Nathan, I felt different. Like a load has been taken off my shoulders. The things she had said about me putting up a wall to protect myself after Dad left bothered me. I have been angry with Dad for so long that I brought other people down with me. My mum, Lindsay, I shouldn't treat them like crap, but I do. It was my way of protecting myself from being hurt, but I was hurting others by being cruel. And there's Nathan. He had liked me for so long, always tried to grab my attention, but I pushed him away. Lindsay said I should be glad someone else likes me. Out of every person who is afraid of me and keeps a distance from me, Nathan doesn't. He acts like he can break whatever force shield I'm hiding from, and he has broken through. Ending up like my mum—heartbroken and a single mother. I don't want someone to walk into my life and make me happy before snatching that happiness away.

I'm not saying that Nathan will be one of those jerks who would date you for a short while, maybe get one thing out of you, and dump you once they have what they want? But what if it was a possibility? I don't know if I could take that heartache.

And now I have confessed everything to the school counsellor, do I tell Lindsay how I felt? It's not so much of a secret to her. We are twins after all. She already knows I'm falling for Nathan. I just need to confess it. If I tell her, will she keep it a secret from everyone? I don't want anyone to know that I may have a crush on Nathan. Lindsay is the type of person who likes to gossip. Our entire grade will know in seconds about me. We are sisters. She wouldn't blab to everyone about my secret, would she? We used to tell each other secrets all the time when we were younger. Yet, I'm still not sure if I should trust her. I'm just uncertain if I'm ready to let the world know how I feel about Nathan. There aren't many people that I can trust until I am ready to admit to Nathan that I like him...

Or even admit it to myself.

What if I tell her and she doesn't believe me, like what I had told her about what Simon had said to me? Or would this be different?

A soft tap on my door interrupts my thoughts.

"Who is it?" I call out.

The door creaks open and Mum pokes her head in. As soon as I saw her, I knew that even if I couldn't talk to Lindsay yet about Nathan, I could talk to Mum.

"Hey," she smiles at me. "I'm just checking up on you."

She stays at the door, unsure if she should enter fully in case I yell at her for coming to my room and bothering me. Normally I would, but today I don't feel like yelling at her. We haven't really spoken since our fight over her engagement. The only time I spoke to her was when I told her I was going out to the concert.

"Mum, can I talk to you?" I ask her. "I need to ask you something."

Mum first looks surprised, but then a smile spreads across her face, and she nods. She opens the door the rest of the way and walks in, coming to sit down on the edge of my bed.

I close my sketchbook and set it down beside me.

Taking a deep breath, I exhale it slowly. I can do this. I shouldn't feel nervous or scared when I talk to my mother about this. That's what she is here for: to listen to what I had to say. She was a teen once herself. She would know what to do about my feelings for Nathan.

"Mum, I know this will sound weird coming from me, but I kind of need boy advice."

Mum's eyes widen. I can't blame her. I never once asked for any advice about boys. It's usually Lindsay who would ask her these questions.

"Sure," she says. "You can ask me anything. Is it about Nathan?"

I bite my lip as I nod. "Is it possible to like someone even if you hate them?"

Mum thinks about it for a second. "Yes, it's possible to be in a hate-love relationship. It's possible to despise someone, yet still find an aspect of them likable." Her lips curl into a smile. "Do you have feelings for Nathan?"

I blush. I tell Mum what I had told Miss Giovanni. She smiles, happy that I took a step toward making progress in liking someone rather than hating them. I still don't understand why she or even Miss Giovanni would even think I'm making progress with my habits. I mean, I'm not. Am I? Just because I have a crush on Nathan, it doesn't mean I want to get friendly with others. Nathan is one person who I like. I still hated everyone else.

"I don't know if I should tell him how I feel," I say. "He knows I don't like him, but he tries so hard to get me to like him. I don't really know how I truly feel at the moment. This feeling I have is overwhelming, and I don't know if it's temporary."

Mum reaches out and pats my shoulder. "Honey, that's all up to you. I can't tell you to do it. You tell him whenever you feel is the right time. And whatever is causing you to be overwhelmed, it's all temporary. Once you figure out your feelings, everything will be okay."

I realise Mum is saying the same things Miss Giovanni had been saying to me today. It still didn't help me with the decision I want to make, though. I still want to know what the right choice is. Is this how you feel when you fall in love or have a crush on someone? Is every decision you make about someone confusing?

"Lindsay already knows I like him. She says I'm in denial. Should I tell her what I feel about Nathan? She said to me today she wanted me to open up to her."

Mum nods, smiling. "And you should do that, Alex. I want you to do it with me too. I'm your mother, and I want you to come to me and tell me what is happening in your life. Not have you shut me out of it. I know you have been angry about everything since your dad left and with Dereck, but I really don't want you to be mad with me. If there is something you want to talk about, tell me. Don't be afraid to open up."

Mum was right. And as much as I hated my sister, there is still a part of me where I miss hanging out with her. We used to talk. Now all we did was backstab each other. We never hang out any more like close sisters do. For the past six years Lindsay has tried to get me to be the close sisters we were, but I didn't want to make the effort. Drifting so far apart since Dad walked out of our lives, I'm not even sure if Lindsay and I can improve our relationship. I miss talking with Mum, too. I miss the mother-daughter stuff we used to do with Lindsay. Now we don't do anything because I refused to be around them. Yet, these are the two people who have been there since Dad left, and all I do is push them away.

But if I tell Lindsay about my crush on Nathan, will she be mad at me? Especially when she likes him too? But even if she does like him, she has Simon. It still makes no sense to me why she has a boyfriend, but secretly sleeps around with other guys. If she isn't happy with Simon, why doesn't she break up with him?

"Is Lindsay around?" I ask.

Mum shakes her head. "Not at the moment. She went to a party."

It wasn't a surprise for me to know she had gone to a party, but it was a school night. Lindsay never goes to a party on a school night. Only Friday nights, and then she spends the whole of Saturday sleeping her hangover off.

"It's a school night," I say.

"Yes, I know. She said it's Eddie's birthday today."

Eddie Olsen. I can't stand him. He is one of my sister's exes who she dated before going steady with Simon. She remains good friends with a lot of her exes.

Mum and I talk for a bit more before she leaves me to be alone. I sit there for a moment, wondering if I should attend this party. Would it be a good idea to go there and talk to Lindsay? Would she want to talk there? Maybe if she wasn't drunk, she would let me. Or maybe I should wait until she returns home. Or maybe I should wait until tomorrow.

Before I think about hesitating, I grab my keys and head to Eddie's. I need to do this before I change my mind.

***

I find a park on the street three houses down from Eddie's. Where I had parked the car, you could hear the music. It's what I don't understand about parties, to why there was a need to play loud music. The night is humid when I head up the path to Eddie's house. I slip my hands into the pockets of my jeans, inhaling a deep breath and exhaling slowly. I can't believe I'm doing this. Maybe this is a stupid idea and I should wait until Lindsay gets home. At the same time I knew if I don't talk to her now, I won't do it later.

When I reached Eddie's house, some guy had already passed out on the grass. I roll my eyes at him. Is it really necessary to drink so much and then pass out later? Where's the fun in that? I head up the front lawn. Three boys and a girl were standing on the veranda, smoking. I didn't recognise any of them. One guy whistles at me, but I don't pay any attention to him. I'm here to find my sister, not to flirt with anyone.

I walk inside. The music is so loud that it vibrates in my ears. I glance around the lounge room for my sister. I can't see her through the drunken bodies of my schoolmates. This honestly doesn't feel like a birthday party. Don't these people realise we have school tomorrow? Why couldn't Eddie wait to celebrate his birthday tomorrow when everyone had Saturday to sleep off their hangover? I push my way through the crowd.

A guy with blue hair approaches me, thinking I'm Lindsay. I don't recognise him as anyone from school. He rubs up against me. I push him into some girls standing behind him. They get annoyed with him. I quickly move away before he comes back over to me.

I couldn't find Lindsay anywhere in the lounge room or corridor. Maybe this is pointless for coming here. What on earth was I thinking to come here expecting to talk to my sister? I should just wait until tomorrow.

But then tomorrow will come, and I probably wouldn't say anything.

"Alex?"

I spin around and see Nathan pushing his way through the crowd towards me. My stomach twists into knots at the sight of him. "Nathan? What are you doing here?"

"I should ask you the same thing. I figured parties weren't your thing."

"Hey, I asked you the question first."

He laughs. "I live next door to Eddie. Eric is here too. We came here hoping to find Eddie and ask him nicely to turn the music down. We have a maths test tomorrow and we want some quiet to study. But I doubt we are going to get any tonight. Nor do the people in our classes even care about their test."

"Why don't you go somewhere else and study?"

He nods. "We could go back to Eric's, but we shouldn't have to go over there because of someone throwing a party."

"I can't find him anywhere," Eric says, joining Nathan and me. "I'm asking around for him, but no one seems to know where he is."

Nathan rolls his eyes. "Great. So I guess we are stuck listening to it all night. I swear someone needs to teach him how to respect his neighbours. How is he even allowed to throw this on a school night?"

Eric rests his hand on Nathan's shoulder. "Hey, it won't be all night. Hopefully not. Maybe someone will call the cops to break this party up." He looks my way, finally noticing that I was here too. His eyes widen when he sees me. "Alex Jennings? What are you doing here?"

"I'm trying to find my sister," I explain. "Have you seen her?"

"I saw her with Simon in the kitchen last time, doing shots. Not sure where she is now."

Cheering comes from the kitchen, along with a few whistles. The three of us make our way towards the kitchen, and that's where I spot Lindsay. Simon has her pressed up against the wall, making out with her. She is only in her bra and skirt. I stand there with my mouth ajar. I have never seen my sister so intoxicated before. Sure, I have seen her stumbling into the house a few times when she was drunk, but this time I don't think she even knew what she was doing, or that she is half naked in the middle of the kitchen in front of everyone. Someone nearby tells them to get a room, and that's when Simon lifts her off the ground, carrying her bridal style. He starts to walk my way.

I narrow my eyes at him and clench my fists together. Oh no, he doesn't. I don't care if they slept together before, but I wasn't going to let Simon carry her off to some room while under the influence. Not when my sister doesn't know what she is doing. Nathan says something to me, but I don't hear him over the music. I walk straight up to Simon before he could carry my sister out of the kitchen. His lips are still on hers, and he doesn't notice me walking towards them. I grab my sister and yank her from his arms. They pull away, confused about what's happening.

"Ow!" Lindsay screams when she plants her feet on the floor. She rubs her arm. She looks my way and narrows her eyes. "What the heck, Alex? Are you trying to break my arm?"

I ignore my sister and turn to Simon.

"Alex?" He stares at me, confused. "What are you doing here?"

"Stay away from my sister, you jerk!" I turn to Lindsay. "The party is over, Lindsay. You're coming home with me."

I grab my sister's wrist, but she pushes me away, stumbling into someone behind her. Someone then comes up behind me and wraps their arms around my waist. My heart races fast.

"What's the matter, Alex?" Simon says. "Why are you leaving so soon? You just got here. Have some fun."

He slips a hand under my shirt, his fingers brushing up against my skin. I don't let him go very far when I grab his wrist and twist his arm. He yelps. Nathan and Eric come to my side. Eric pulls me away as Nathan punches Simon in his jaw.

"Never touch Alex again!" he warns Simon.

Simon chuckles. "Why do you care so much about that bitch, anyway? She's just a waste of air. I suggested to her to disappear and to put herself out of misery."

When Simon said that to me the other day, it stung. But this time he was saying it in front of everyone, and that hurt more. Did everyone agree with Simon that I should put myself out of misery? Does Lindsay agree with him?

But thankfully, not everyone agrees with him.

"Alex is not a waste of air," Nathan tells him. "Don't ever say that about her again, or tell her to disappear."

Nathan hits Simon in the jaw again. Simon tries to hit him back, but Nathan's reflexes are faster than his. He throws another punch, this time knocking Simon off his feet. I stare at Nathan, my heart fluttering in my chest. I couldn't believe he just fought another guy for me, even though I'm sure I would be okay with handling Simon on my own.

"Why the heck did you do that for?" Lindsay demands, her words slurring as she hits Nathan hard in the chest.

Nathan doesn't flinch when my sister hits him. He grabs my sister by her arms. "Lindsay, I'm sorry, but I had to. He was trying to feel Alex up, and had said some horrible things to her."

Before she can respond, I grab my sister's arm. Nathan drops his hands from her, and I began dragging her towards the door. She screams at me to let her go, trying to free herself from my grip. It only makes me tighten my grip. A few people turn their heads to see what was happening.

"Hey, where are you going with Lindsay?" Eddie asks as he bumps into us on the way out. In his hand is Lindsay's shirt. I snatch it from him.

"I'm taking Lindsay home," I tell him.

"Oh, come on, Alex. Don't be a buzzkill. Why don't you and Lindsay stay longer?"

"She doesn't want to stay," Nathan steps in. "Now, if you don't mind, could you please turn the music down? Have some respect for your neighbours."

Eddie laughs, as if whatever Nathan said was a joke. "It's my party, mate. I'm not turning it down." He walks off.

Lindsay tries to break free again. I tighten my grip, ignoring the insults she spits out at me. I drag her out the front door. As soon as we step onto the front lawn, she shoves me hard. I let go of her and Lindsay makes a run for it.

"Lindsay!" I shout at her.

Eric and Nathan take off after her as she runs around the front yard. Just as they reach her, Lindsay drops to her knees near the garden and vomits. I walk over to them, telling the guys if they mind leaving me alone with my sister for a second. They walk over to the footpath, watching us closely.

Lindsay stands up and faces me, her eyes narrowing at me.

"See," I say. "This is exactly why you shouldn't drink at parties. Horrible things happen to you."

Lindsay rolls her eyes. "Oh my gosh, no they don't, Alex!"

"Yes, they do. You should thank me for getting you out of there. God knows what Simon would do to you."

She gestures to herself, her voice slurring as she speaks. "*I* should thank you?" Lindsay laughs and snatches her shirt from me, putting it back on. "I don't need to thank you for anything, Alex. You love ruining my life, don't you? Little Miss Perfect, who does nothing wrong, and wants to hate everyone. You can't tell me what to do. There's nothing wrong with having a little fun."

I roll my eyes. Lindsay loved reminding me this, and I hated it. As her older sister, it was my job to protect her from screwing up her life! It's not like I even care what she does, but I do care because I am her sister.

"I was trying to stop you from doing something stupid that could ruin your life!" I tell her.

"Why do you care what I get up to? I'm not the one who hates everything and everyone. Just because you hate parties, it doesn't mean you can stop me from going to one."

"Whatever. You're drunk. Anything can happen to you. What if you got pregnant? What if the neighbours call the police? You'll be in so much trouble for drinking. You do realise that we don't turn eighteen until June."

Lindsay laughs like all of this is a big joke. "So what if I'm underage? You can't stop me from drinking. Do you want to know why you don't drink? Or even have fun once in a while, Alex? It's because you're a pathetic loser who doesn't have a life. All you want to do is sit around and hate everything and everyone. What kind of life do you live, anyway?"

Tears pricked my eyes, and I did everything to hold them back. I can't let my sister see the tears. She will laugh at me. Another excuse for her to call me a pathetic loser. I try to remind myself that she is drunk and probably doesn't know what she is talking about, but then again the truth comes out when you're intoxicated. Maybe she is right. I am a pathetic loser. What kind of person am I if I keep holding onto my dad, thinking he will return home when I know he never will? What kind of person am I for hating everyone and everything, all so I don't get hurt or feel guilty for doing something that makes me think of Dad? Or so I can protect myself from being hurt again the next time someone leaves? Is it even normal to feel like this?

Maybe it isn't normal, but I wanted to protect myself. How much pain does someone need to go through when someone they love leaves them? Someone who is supposed to love you in return, but doesn't? I hate everything, so nothing could remind me of Dad. Hate is a powerful emotion. If I hate the person who walks out of my life, I will be okay because I won't feel anything once they're gone. Their soul will be dead to me.

Wouldn't it?

"This isn't about me, Lindsay. This is about you being drunk and being in a dangerous situation. What happens if a guy forces themselves onto you, and you end up pregnant? Do you have any idea what you were doing in there when Simon was all over you?"

"Of course I know what I was doing in there, Alex. Simon and I have had sex before. We have been doing it for a while. We use protection, so you do not need to worry about me."

I frown. "You shouldn't be having sex with that jerk."

"Oh, shut up, Alex. Just because you don't like to have fun doesn't mean I can't. I can do whatever I want and you can't stop me."

I stand there staring at my sister. There were a million things I wanted to say to her, but there was no point. She won't listen. She is too stubborn. Whatever happens, I hope she doesn't plan on getting into a car with a drunk driver on the way home from the party.

Without another word, I turn, walking towards the path where Eric and Nathan stood.

"Yes, get out of here, you pathetic loser!" Lindsay screams at me. "Nobody wants you here! And Simon is right, you're a waste of air!"

I walk straight past Nathan and Eric, heading down the street. Tears stream down my face. The boys hurried after me, asking me if I'm okay. I nod, wiping my eyes. Of course I wasn't okay, but I didn't need them to comfort me or have any sympathy after what Lindsay said to me. What hurts the most is her agreeing with Simon that I was just a waste of air.

Their words circle my head repeated. I'm a waste of air and a pathetic loser who hangs on hope that my father will someday return. I wanted everything to go back to normal, when I knew it never would. Rather than taking out my anger in another way, I take it out on others.

"Where is your car parked, Alex?" Nathan asks me.

"Just up here somewhere," I say.

"Go with her, Nathan," Eric says. "I will go inside. I will tell your parents that you are helping a friend."

Nathan thanks him, and he walks alongside me. I didn't want him to, but he did. Thankfully, it's dark out and he can't see the tears that are in my eyes. I don't think the few streetlights that are on will show the tears. I feel like a fool for trying to help my sister back there. Maybe it's best I don't tell her about my crush on Nathan at all. She doesn't deserve to know anything.

What was I even thinking to come here and hope to pull her aside so we could talk?

We walk in silence. The music from the house still reached down the street. I want to get out of here and forget I even came here.

"Nathan, do you think I'm a waste of air?" I almost whispered it, as if I were afraid to say it out loud. "Or a pathetic loser?"

Nathan puts a hand on my shoulder. "Don't listen to them. It's not true, Alex."

"But I am what they say, aren't I?"

We stop walking for a moment, and Nathan makes me look at him.

"No. You aren't, Alex. No one is. They have no right to say those words to you. Don't let them get to you."

I give him a small smile. "Thanks."

I turn and kept walking down the street.

"I'm sorry about Lindsay," Nathan says.

"Don't be sorry. There is no need for you to be sorry. Oh, thank you for pulling Simon away from me. I didn't expect you to do that."

He chuckles. "Yes, well, I wasn't expecting myself to do that either. I didn't like him putting his hands on you. He shouldn't have done that. Or have said those things to you."

We reach my car.

I wipe my eyes as more tears escaped my eyes. "Well, goodnight, Nathan."

I turn to my car when he stops me.

"Hey, do you want to go somewhere and get coffee?" he asks.

"I don't drink coffee."

He stares at me, his eyes widening. "You don't drink coffee? How do you not drink it? I can't live without it."

"I just can. I can't stand the taste. Anyway, I doubt there will be any coffee shops open at this time of night."

"You're right. There's none opened at eight o'clock. But there's McDonald's we can grab the coffee from. Maybe we could catch a late-night movie."

"We have school tomorrow. Plus, I need to be home before ten thirty."

"McDonald's it is then."

I smile, and we get into my car.

Chapter 19

It was after eight thirty when we settled down at a table at the nearest McDonald's. The only people who were at the restaurant tonight were us, a family of four seated near the restroom, and a gentleman in his late forties seated in front of the plasma TV mounted on the wall, watching some drama TV show that was playing.

I'd ordered myself a chocolate thick shake. Rather than ordering a coffee, Nathan had ordered a strawberry sundae.

I take a sip of the shake; the ice cream melting instantly on my tongue. "Mmm, I forgot how good these things taste. I don't remember the last time I was here."

"Really? How come you haven't come here for so long?" He takes a spoonful of his ice cream.

I tuck a strand of hair that escaped my ponytail behind my ear. "My mum doesn't order much takeout. I could still come here on my own, I guess, but I haven't been able to bring myself to a lot of places since…"

I pause. Did I really want to tell him about Dad? I mean, there are many families where a parent had walked out on them. I shouldn't feel ashamed for what had happened. It's just I don't know if I want to share that piece of personal information with him yet. He doesn't even need to know what happened in my family. I don't know if I'm able to trust him with the secrets I had about turning against everyone. Would he say I'm being ridiculous for turning against everyone after my dad left? Or would he tell me to get over myself and move on like Lindsay would?

"Since what?" Nathan wants to know.

I look at him. He will listen, won't he? He wouldn't judge me or anything about Dad leaving my family. No, I can't tell him just yet. I'm not ready to discuss this kind of stuff with him. I can tell Miss Giovanni, but there are still some things I haven't told her either. There are just some things I want to keep to myself and not tell anyone. No one needs to know.

"It's nothing," I answer.

Nathan put his spoon down in his ice cream and reaches across the table, putting his hand over mine. I jump at his touch. "Alex, you can tell me."

I stare at our hands. His hands looked so perfect as they fitted over mine. For a second I wondered what it would be like if we interlaced our hands together.

I swiftly move my hand away from him before I even realise what I was thinking about. Maybe Nathan wanted this affection with me or he wanted me to open up to him, but I wasn't ready for either of it. Damn it. I don't even know what I'm supposed to be doing about my crush on him.

I place my hands around my drink. Without glancing at Nathan, I say, "I know you want to know, but I don't know if I should tell you."

"Why is that?"

I force myself to look at him. "I just don't feel ready to open up."

He nods, pressing his lips into a thin line. "Okay, whenever you feel ready to tell me, I will listen."

I give him a small smile, glad he wasn't pushing me to do anything. He returns the smile, which makes butterflies dance in my stomach. He breaks eye contact with me and turns back to his sundae, and scoops some ice cream into his mouth.

He gestures to the sundae. "Would you like some ice cream?"

I shake my head. "No thanks, Nathan. You can have it all to yourself."

We sit there in silence for a few minutes with Nathan eating his sundae and me sipping on my drink.

Nathan breaks the silence first. "So how's it going with your mother's fiancé?"

I frown. Does he really have to bring up Dereck? "What about him?"

"Are you getting along with him now after what happened when you found out your mother was getting married?"

I shake my head. "No. We still aren't getting along. We may never will. I just don't like him. I feel like he is trying to take over my family."

"I completely understand. It took me a while to accept both of my parents' decision to remarry. I live with my dad and stepmum. I see my mum and stepdad every other weekend. It sucks to see your parents remarry someone else, but then just seeing them happy is all that matters. In some ways, I was like you, Alex."

I stare at him, confused. "Like me? How?"

"My parents divorced when I was ten. I was angry at the world, thinking maybe it was my fault they were ending their marriage, even when they said it wasn't. For a while, I was disruptive in school and my grades were horrible as I tried to figure out what went wrong with my parents. My dad took me to a boxing class, and it helped me to manage my anger and eventually accept their decision to remarry. So if you ever need to talk about anything, just let me know. I am here for you, Alex. And if you want help with letting go of some anger, you could always come boxing with me. I box a few times a week."

I give him a small smile, surprised to hear he has gone through something similar to me. I just couldn't work out how he could get his anger out of control when I couldn't control mine. No matter what happened between my parents, I don't think I could ever fully accept their decision. Nor could I accept Mum marrying Dereck.

Looking away, I sip my drink.

"Can I ask what happened with your dad?" Nathan asks.

I freeze when he asks me that question. What do I tell him? Do I tell him the truth about what really happened?

I glance at my watch. "Could we please go?"

"You're a private person, aren't you?"

I nod. "There are some things that not everyone needs to know about."

Nathan watches me carefully. He doesn't question me on anything else. "Let me finish the rest of this, and we can go."

I wait for him to finish his ice cream, and then we went to the car. I drive him back home, pulling into the driveway. The party was still going on. I wonder how much longer they are going to be. I guess half of them won't be showing up at school tomorrow, or if they do, they will come with hangovers.

I wonder if Lindsay was still here.

"Thanks for tonight," I say.

He smiles. "No problems. I will see you tomorrow."

I nod. He takes off his seatbelt. He was about to get out when he turns to me.

"Alex?"

"Yeah?"

"Can I kiss you?"

I swallow hard, not sure if I felt comfortable with it. What if someone from the party sees us?

Curious about what it would be like to kiss him, I nod.

Nathan reaches over and strokes my cheek with his thumb. We stare at each other for what felt like an eternity. The butterflies dance around my stomach. He leans forward slowly to kiss me. My heart races in my chest, and I panic. I can't do this. Someone will see us.

I pivot my head before our lips touch.

"Alex?"

"I'm sorry." I don't dare to look at him. Will he understand why I can't kiss him right now? "I can't kiss you right now. Not yet."

He nods. "I understand."

No, you don't understand. I shouldn't even think about wanting to kiss you.

We sit still for a second in silence.

"I will see you tomorrow, okay?" Nathan breaks the silence, reaching for the door handle.

I nod. "Yeah, I will see you tomorrow."

"Goodnight, Alex."

"Goodnight, Nathan."

He gets out of the car. I watch him walk to the front door of his house before I put the gear into reverse, pulling out of the driveway. I drive home, thinking about Nathan.

It's not until I'm halfway home that I feel stupid for allowing him to kiss me, but then back out of the whole idea. Why did I do that? Why did I say yes to it if I wasn't even ready for it?

Then I realise what I really need to do before I kiss him. I have to tell him my secret. I have to tell him about Dad. It's the only way I can allow myself to move on and be happy. If Miss Giovanni says that I distance myself and don't have fun because of my issues with Dad leaving, then I need to figure out how to move on. I need to tell myself that everything is okay. Dad may have left, but it doesn't mean I should stop myself from having fun or falling in love just because I'm afraid of ending up like Mum. I can't let what happened with Dad ruin my life from a choice he had made.

Tomorrow. I will tell him tomorrow. I don't know if I want to be in a relationship with Nathan, but I need to take a risk. Without trying, I'll never know how Nathan will react. Maybe nothing will happen. Maybe I'm panicking for nothing.

Chapter 20

It was no surprise that Lindsay returned home later, missing her curfew by an hour. I wasn't even sure if Mum knew or was still up. I could hear my sister vomiting in the bathroom shortly after she got into the house, keeping me up. Half of me wanted to check on her to make sure she was alright, but I'm sure she wouldn't want me to. Checking up on her will only lead us into another argument over what happened earlier tonight.

Of course, she did not come down for breakfast the next day. Mum had to check on her to make sure she was up. She told Mum she wasn't hungry. I'm sure she just didn't want Mum to question her on why she was hungover, or even wanted to face me. I don't think Mum knows she missed curfew, and Lindsay was probably trying to avoid Mum finding out that she'd been drinking. Mum would never approve of her behaviour.

Lindsay didn't come downstairs until Mum left for work. Neither of us mentioned anything from last night. We didn't say one word to each other. She's probably still pissed at me for embarrassing her at the party. Or maybe she was in no mood because of her hangover.

Once at school, my sister and I go our separate ways until roll call. English was the first period. I watch Lindsay from where I was sitting two seats down from her. I chuckle to myself. She kept rubbing her temples throughout the lesson, not being able to concentrate on anything Mrs Callea was saying. That will teach her to drink so much.

When there were a few minutes left to the end of the lesson, Lindsay decided she couldn't take the hangover anymore and asked Mrs Callea if she could go down to the sick bay. My teacher allows her to go. She picks up her belongings and walks out of the classroom.

Once the bell rings, everyone gathers up their belongings and rushes out of the door to their next class. I take my time packing my things. Nathan is near me. I need to talk to him before he disappears, as I don't have any other classes with him today. I also didn't want to approach him in the corridors or at lunch with no one seeing us together.

"Remember your essay is due on Friday, so please do not forget it," Mrs Callea reminds the students who are still in the classroom. "Alex, could you please remind your sister about the essay?"

Whatever, I wanted to say. Why should I remind her when Mrs Callea should be the one to tell Lindsay about her schoolwork? Besides, it's not like she will listen to me.

I nod. "Yeah, sure, Mrs Callea."

Nathan turns to leave, and I hurry after him. I grab his arm and pull him aside as the rest of the class left the classroom.

"Can I please talk to you for a second?" I ask him, hoping he didn't mind being a few minutes late to his next class.

Nathan nods. From the corner of my eye, I notice Mrs Callea watching me carefully, probably making sure I don't use any kind of violence with Nathan like I did last time.

I wait until our teacher leaves the classroom and we are completely alone. I closed the door so no one outside could see me talking to Nathan as they walked by, or hear what I had to say.

Nathan turns to me. "Is everything okay?"

I nod. "Yeah. I... Are you doing anything tonight?"

Nathan thinks for a moment and then shakes his head. "No, I don't think so. Why?"

"I want to see you tonight. I want to tell you something. Could you please meet me at the park around eight? I will be near the playground."

He nods. "Yeah, I can do that. I will be there."

"Come alone. Don't bring anyone with you."

He nods. "Of course. I will see you tonight."

He gives me a smile before we go our separate ways.

As I head to my next class, I imagine how it will go with him tonight, telling him everything about my dad. I don't know how he will react, and I wonder if he will really listen like he said he would. Half of me feared he was going to run off and disappear when he hears about my past; the other half knew he will listen. Whatever fears I had that kept me from being close to anyone, I can trust Nathan. He has listened to me about how I felt about Mum being engaged to Dereck. He will listen to me tonight. I needed to get this off my chest and explain to Nathan about everything. From why I am the way I am, why I fight with my sister, why I freaked out at Splash Resort, and why I couldn't kiss him last night. After everything he has done for me, he deserved an explanation.

I only hope I don't back out and let my fears get the better of me when I see him again.

***

I almost hesitated about meeting Nathan as it got closer to eight o'clock. Was I making the right decision? Once I tell Nathan everything, there is no turning back. I need to tell him. I can't leave him in the dark forever.

I tell Mum I'm going out for a walk and that I shouldn't be too long. The sun is setting, turning the sky with shades of red, orange, and yellow. It should be dark by the time I get to the park.

I get here before Nathan does, walking over to the playground where I had told him I would be.

I can tell Nathan this, I say to myself as I walk over to the swing. *He listened before, so he will listen again. He won't judge me. There is no reason for me to worry.*

I sit down on a swing, rocking myself slowly back and forward while I waited, twisting my bracelets. It's almost completely dark. Will Nathan be here soon? He wouldn't stand me up, would he? I'm the only person in this deserted park. My heart races as I look around, hoping I won't be out here for too long on my own. While I waited for Nathan, I let my mind wander, rehearsing in my head what I will say when he gets here. I'm lost in my thoughts when Nathan arrives. I don't notice him until he sits down on the swing beside me. He says nothing, just waits for me to speak. I stop swinging, staring at the ground. I can't look at him. It will make me nervous if I do. Maybe even avoid telling him what I want to say.

"Do you really want to know why I hate everything and everyone?" I ask him.

He nods. "Yes, I do. It will help me understand why you act the way you do."

"Promise me you won't tell anyone once I tell you." This time I glance up at him. He watches me carefully. "Not even Eric."

"I promise."

I turn away from Nathan, looking at the ground. I feel his eyes on me, waiting for me to begin.

I take a deep breath and exhale it slowly. *You can do this, Alex. Just pretend you're talking to Miss Giovanni.*

"It all started on Lindsay's and my twelfth birthday. We woke up to find Mum crying in the kitchen. She wiped it off like it was nothing and told us not to worry, that she didn't want us to ruin our birthday. But then we realised Dad was nowhere in the house. We thought maybe he was out getting a last minute present for us. Our friends were arriving soon, and we thought maybe he would return home before the party started. He didn't. Mum tried to put on a brave face for us, but something wasn't right."

I pause. *Keep going, Alex. You're doing well.*

"Growing up, I was close to my father. We did everything together. Rather than joining my sister and our friends at the party, I sat outside on the steps, waiting for him to return home. Only he never came home. I figure maybe he got held up somewhere. Mum waited the next day to tell us that Dad had walked out on us. He was never coming back. I never wanted to believe her. I wanted to believe he would come home.

"As the days went by, I refused to do anything except sit on the steps and wait for him. I would sit out there no matter what the weather was, come rain or shine. I didn't care if I got sick from sitting out in the rain, just as long as he came home safely. Depression took over me. I was confused about why he had left us. Over time, Lindsay and I grew apart. We would get into fights over unnecessary things. That's when I started hating everyone."

I pause for a moment to take a breath. I expected Nathan to interrupt and say something, but he didn't. "The reason I choose to hate everyone is so I could protect myself from being hurt when the next person left. I figured if I set up a wall around myself, that the next time someone was to leave, I wouldn't feel any kind of emotion towards them. The reason I hate you is because what if I got close to you and then you left? I don't want to experience the heartbreak my mum had when Dad left. Not only did I decide to hate everything, but I did the same thing with the things I enjoy. It only reminded me of Dad. I didn't want to be reminded of the fun times. Sometimes it feels wrong to have fun without him. The only thing I still like to do that I used to do with my dad is drawing. Drawing calms me and allows me to express how I feel. That day when we went to Splash Resort, I had a panic attack while we were there. It was like the moment I was having fun with you, the attack came on to remind me what I shouldn't be doing."

The tears prickle my eyes. I allow them to fall. Nathan reaches out and grabs my hand, pulling me closer to him. I sit on his lap, and he puts an arm around my waist to hold me.

"You're the first guy to ask me out because no other guy would dare to ask me, afraid of what I might do to them. When you asked me, it made me think about my parents, how my dad left my mum. I don't want to be with a guy if they were to leave. I don't want to be like my parents. I want to be with someone whom I can love. Not be with for a short time, but forever. I don't enjoy talking about how I feel about my dad. So instead of talking about him, I draw pictures of him in my book to express my feelings, taking old photos and reliving the memories that I want to hold on forever. I still hold on to the hope that he will return home. People tell me to let him go, but I don't know how to. Sometimes I think my mum knows where he is, but she won't tell me or Lindsay. I really hate her for getting remarried. What if Dereck is like my dad and he leaves too? I don't want to see my mum go through another heartbreak. Sometimes I wonder if my dad has ever loved me or even my sister."

We sit there in silence as I sob. Nathan runs a hand up and down my back, which instantly soothes me. He pulls me into a hug. As he hugged me, it was like all the emotions I had kept to myself over the years were finally gone. Relief washes over me.

"I'm sorry, Alex," he says.

I pull away from the hug, wiping my eyes. "You don't need to be sorry."

"I know." He strokes my hair. "Thank you for telling me everything. That's a lot of weight for you to carry. And Alex, I want you to know that there is no need to be afraid of me. I will not leave you like your father did."

I stay silent, unsure how I should answer. How do I know if he means what he said? Wouldn't anyone say those exact words to get you to trust them before stabbing you in the back later?

"Do you allow anyone to see your drawings?" he wants to know.

"Only Miss Giovanni has seen them. I don't really trust anyone seeing them. I feel others will judge me if they see them."

"Would you trust me? I would like to see the drawings if it's okay."

I stare at him. Could I trust him to see my drawings? Do I really want him to see them? If I show him, what will he think of them? Not just of my dad, but of the picture I had drawn of him? Would he like the drawings, or would he disapprove them because I did it without his permission?

"I will only show you them if you promise me not to tell anyone about them," I answer.

Nathan nods. "I promise."

Nathan drives us back to my house, but I make him park his car a couple of houses up from mine. I didn't want Mum or Lindsay to see his car.

I open the front door quietly. I hear Mum humming in the kitchen to music. Calling out to Mum to let her know I'm home, Nathan quietly sneaks into the house behind me. Before Mum could come in and see Nathan, I dragged him up the stairs to my room. The last thing I wanted was for Mum to see him and ask questions I don't want to answer. We sneak past my sister's room and enter mine.

As soon as I closed the door to my room, my heart flutters in my chest. Was it because I was alone in my room with Nathan? I have never had a guy in my room before. Or maybe I was terrified of Mum or Lindsay finding Nathan in here. Or maybe it was because I was about to show someone other than Miss Giovanni my drawings.

Especially when one drawing was of him.

Nathan glances around my room. It's a little messy with a few of my clothes on the floor that I haven't yet put in the hamper. A few of my art supplies were on the floor as well, some of them on my desk. My room is pretty plain; not a single poster was up on my deep purple walls. I'm sure in any other teenage girl's room there would be at least a couple of posters of celebrity crushes, but I wasn't like other teenage girls. Especially Lindsay, who had dozens of posters of Harry Styles and other celebrity posters on her walls.

I walk over to my bed and grab my sketchbook from under the pillow. Taking a deep breath, I turn to Nathan. He is standing in the middle of my room, watching me. I hand him the book. He takes it and flips through it. I fidget with my hands as I wait for him to say what he thought. My palms are sweaty. I wipe them on my jeans.

From his facial expression, Nathan seemed impressed with how well I could draw; his eyes widened.

"These are really great. Have you ever entered an art competition?" Nathan asks me.

"No. Mrs Hawkins has recently asked me to enter one, but I said no. My artwork is kind of personal and I don't want anyone to see it."

"Are you sure? These are really good. I reckon if you entered one, you would definitely win first place."

"I'm positive."

Nathan stops and stares at something. He then glances up at me, his eyes widening. My heart skips a beat. He is at the drawing of him.

"You drew me?"

I nod, blushing, biting my lip.

"Wow. No one has drawn me like this so well."

I give him a shy smile. "Thanks."

Nathan closes the book, handing it back to me. I take it and place it back under the pillow before walking back over to him. I figure that now is probably the perfect time to come clean and tell him exactly how I feel about him.

God, I wish this nervous feeling would go away.

"Nathan, I need to tell you something."

"What is it?"

"I-I..."

"What? You can tell me, Alex."

"I like you. Really like you."

Nathan smiles, and the butterflies flutter in my stomach as I give him a shy smile in return. We stare at each other, neither of us making a move or saying anything. There's a gap between us, and I wanted to change that. I wanted to kiss him the way I should have done last night.

I take a step closer to him, telling myself that I'm ready to do this. I will not let my fear of falling in love get the better of me. And I'm definitely not going to let Dad stop me from living my life. How many opportunities would I lose if I don't take a chance?

Nathan tilts his head towards me, gently placing his lips on mine. My heart races fast, and a million thoughts race through my head. I try not to panic as we kiss, worried about getting busted with someone walking in and seeing me receive my first kiss from someone I'm supposed to hate. He kissed me slowly. He doesn't use tongue or force the kiss onto me. The kiss is gentle.

Lindsay is the one person I'm worried about walking in on me than I am of Mum finding out that I have a boy in my room. If Lindsay finds me in here with Nathan, there is no doubt she will tell everyone she knew that I, Alexander Madeline Jennings, had kissed Nathan. Throughout high school everyone has known me for hating them. What will people think if they knew I was kissing a guy who I'm supposed to hate?

And then I remember.

The door!

I quickly push Nathan off me.

"What?" Nathan says, confused. "Did I do something wrong? Was the kiss too fast for you?"

I walk over to the door. "You didn't do anything. The kiss was fine." I lock the door. No one can get in now. I walk back over to Nathan. "I'm just locking the door so no one will walk in, especially Lindsay."

I move closer to Nathan, my body craving to kiss him again. Nathan closes the gap between us, cupping his hands on my jaw. I wrap my arms around his neck. There's a nauseous feeling in the pit of my stomach, but I ignore it. I want to enjoy this moment rather than thinking about my fears.

As I kissed him, I knew I wasn't making a mistake at all.

Chapter 21

For the first time, I couldn't stop smiling when I woke up the next morning. I couldn't remember the last time I ever smiled.

And it felt so good.

I bounce into the kitchen, humming happily to myself. I grab a bowl of cereal and sat down at the table. Lindsay and Mum walk in shortly afterwards. Mum does a double take when she sees the smile on my face.

"You seem happy this morning, Alex," she says, walking over to the jug and switches it on to. "Did you sleep well?"

"I slept well, thanks," I reply.

Lindsay stands at the fridge, watching me, as if she was completely dumbfounded on who I am. Of course I knew I was feeling great for once because of Nathan, and I know she was going to want to know everything that was going on.

Mum and Lindsay made their breakfast and then came to sit down at the table. Lindsay sits across from me, narrowing her eyes at me, trying to figure out what was going on with me. I wanted to tell her and Mum everything about last night, but I wanted to keep having Nathan being here last night a secret. Questions will arise, and I wasn't sure if I was ready to announce how I felt towards him. Even though the other night I was ready to tell Lindsay, but her drunken self probably wouldn't have remembered anything I had said. Mum, I wasn't ready to inform her yet. Plus, I didn't want to be in trouble for sneaking a boy into my room without Mum's consent. All Nathan and I did was kiss. Nothing else. So there was no reason for her to worry.

"Girls, Dereck and I are going out tonight," Mum announces to us at the table. "You will have the house to yourselves."

"Great!" Lindsay says. "I hope you have a good night."

Mum smiles. "Thank you, Lindsay. Just promise me, girls, that there won't be any fighting while I am gone."

"We won't, Mum," Lindsay says.

Mum and Lindsay turn to me. Both of them wait for me to say something nasty about Dereck. I would, but right now Nathan was all I could think about.

When we finish eating, Mum cleans up our dishes, and I head out to finish getting ready for school. Lindsay follows me out.

"What's going on with you, Alex?" Lindsay asks me once we get to the stairs.

"Nothing is going on," I say.

"Something *is* wrong."

I stop and turn to her halfway up the staircase. I should be able to open up and tell her everything about last night. My first kiss, I was dying to tell her. But after the things my sister said the other night, I couldn't tell her yet.

"Nothing is wrong," I tell her. "Can't I be happy?"

Lindsay raises her eyebrows. "I'm not saying you can't. It's just that it's not like you to be so happy."

I turn around, unsure what to tell her without letting her know what had happened between Nathan and me last night. Instead of mentioning Nathan, I said the words I never expected I'd say: "Maybe I have changed."

***

As much as I wanted to keep on smiling once I got to school, I had to stop. Even though Nathan is all I could think about, I didn't want everyone asking me questions. Although I'm sure Lindsay will fill them all in about my behaviour, how she wasn't buying the fact that I have changed my ways. I saw Nathan in the corridor on my way to roll call. We smile at each other, but say nothing. I didn't want to look suspicious talking to him like what happened the other day when Lindsay caught me.

I didn't have class with him until third period. I sit in my usual spot, watching Nathan as we wait for Mr

Brown, who apparently hasn't shown up for class yet. No one is complaining that he hasn't turned up yet. He was probably held up in the staffroom. Nathan snuck a few glances at me while he talked to Eric.

Thank goodness my sister isn't in this class. She would immediately want to know what's going on between Nathan and me.

The class soon quiets down, settling ourselves into our seats as our principal walks into the classroom instead of our usual teacher.

"Good morning everyone," Mr Matthews greets us as he stood at the front of the classroom.

We greet him back.

"Where's Mr Brown?" Eric speaks for the entire class. "Are we having you as our teacher today?"

Mr Matthews shakes his head. "No, I will not be taking the class today. Mr Brown is off sick. We could not organise a substitute for him today. So I'm going to allow you to have a free period."

The class breaks into a cheer about having a free period.

Instead of joining in on the cheer, I glance over at Nathan, whose eyes lock with mine and smiles. I return it.

Getting up from their seats, our classmates hurry out of the classroom, heading to the library, which Mr Matthews had directed us to spend the lesson there, where the librarian would watch us. Mr Matthews follows them out. I should follow out too, but I ask Nathan if we can hang back for a bit before we join the rest of the class. Eric leaves, telling us he will meet us in the library.

My stomach twists into knots. I wonder if Nathan had told him about us.

"How much does Eric know about us?" I ask as I set my bag down at my feet and sit down on a desk.

Nathan walks over to me. "He knows about the concert. I haven't told him about Splash Resort yet. Don't be mad with me, but I told him about last night. He has promised not to tell anyone about us. I thought it was only right to tell him because he was the one who had been helping me with ways to ask you out."

"Does anyone else know about us?"

Nathan shakes his head. "No. I told Eric only. I'm not planning to tell anyone else unless you want me to. Like I said, I only told him because I thought he had the right to know. He was the one who helped me ask you out. He even told me I was insane for wanting to go out with you. And no, I haven't told him about your secret."

The knot in my stomach tightens. Of course Eric knows about us, especially when he told Nathan to go with me after the party the other night. I don't know Eric well. How do I know if Nathan is telling the truth or if Eric will keep his promise? It's bad enough I feel uncomfortable sneaking around with Nathan.

"Nathan, I appreciate it if you didn't tell Eric everything that goes on between us. The one thing I'm afraid of doing at the moment is sneaking around with you, hoping no one finds out about our relationship."

Nathan moves closer to me, stroking my hair that hangs loose around my shoulders. "Hey. Who cares what others say? We can date."

"Yeah, but I'm known for hating the world. If I go out with you, people will think there is something wrong with me. They will make fun of me for wanting to be with you."

Nathan touches the side of my cheek. His touch makes my skin tingle. "People change, Alex. You can change what you feel about someone. That's what you're doing. You're trying to get out of the habit of hating people. You're trying to move on and let go of your fears of the past. If no one wants to understand and wants to be judgmental, that's too bad for them. Don't let others control your thinking on what you want to do."

I nod, knowing he was right. But it was hard to think positively when people can be judgmental about the kind of person you are and who you want to be with.

Nathan goes on. "Just remember, Alex, that as long as you're happy with yourself, that's all that matters."

I give Nathan a half smile. His words instantly make me feel better about myself. But I still felt afraid of people knowing about my relationship with Nathan. I'm still trying to get to know this new feeling of being with someone, and I don't even know if I'm ready for it.

But Nathan is right. Who cares what others say if I'm dating him? It's none of their concern if I'm dating him or not. As long as I feel happy with myself, that's the only thing that should matter.

Nathan presses his lips against mine. I wrap my arms around his neck. My heart races when he rests his hands on my waist, but the panic feeling swiftly disappears. When we pull apart, he takes my hand and we go to join the rest of our class before we get into trouble for not being in the library.

Chapter 22

The moment I walked onto the school grounds the next day, I couldn't help but notice immediately that something was wrong. You know those nightmares where you're walking down a corridor, and people stand on the side, pointing and laughing at you? Only this wasn't a dream. No one was pointing and laughing at me. They were whispering.

I think back to this morning, how my sister kept smirking at me before we left the house. Like she knew something I didn't.

The first thought that comes to me is: What did Lindsay do?

Thoughts race through my head, wondering what everyone could say about me. They are talking about me, aren't they? I'm so used to people saying horrible things about me, or keeping a distance from me. I ignore them only. It's what I do. But now I'm dating Nathan, I felt exposed, like everyone knew about it.

My heart races. What if someone knows about Nathan and me? Did anyone see us last night?

I sit outside the library, burying my head in my sketchbook, wanting the ground to open up and swallow me whole. Anything to stop people from staring and whispering at me. I take a couple of breaths as I feel a panic attack coming on. I can't let anyone see me like this. Nathan may have told me not to worry about what others say, but I can't help thinking what they will say. They would probably say it's about time I got a boyfriend. Or maybe they would say it's about time I stopped hating on everyone. I don't know if I can take the things they say. I used to never really worry about what others say, but since getting feelings towards Nathan, it's like he has cut through my emotions. I let down the guard I had up to protect me for these last six years. Now, all I feel is paranoia about what people think, and the names Lindsay calls me have become more hurtful than ever before.

And I know exactly what Lindsay will say about Nathan and me.

"Alex?" Nathan calls my name.

I look up to see him and Eric walking over to me. The panic attack worsens when I see them. My chest tightens and I couldn't breathe. I closed my sketchbook, getting up from the seat and moved. I can't be near Nathan right now.

"Alex, we need to talk," Nathan says, grabbing my arm before I could escape.

"I-I can't talk to you." I can feel everyone's eyes on me as they walk by.

Nathan pulls me inside the building and into an empty classroom. Eric follows us, closing the door, making sure no one sees us. Especially a teacher.

"People know about us, don't they?" I ask.

He nods. My head spins, and the nauseous begins. I clutch my hand over my stomach and sit down. No. People can't know. How did anyone see us together? I made sure no one knew.

Nathan kneels in front of me and tells me to breathe and take deep breaths to steady my panic attack. I listen to him.

Once Nathan has helped me to calm down, Eric says, "Someone posted online about you liking Nathan."

The first person who comes to my mind is Lindsay. She's the only person who would do this to me. It will be payback for liking Nathan because she couldn't get what she wants.

"Lindsay." My breathing speeds up again. "Lindsay is the only person who would tell."

Eric nods. "It was Lindsay."

"How did she find out?"

Nathan places his hands on my shoulders. "Breathe, Alex. Breathe."

I take a couple of deep breaths to calm down, and I'm soon able to breathe normally again.

For now, until I panic again.

"You and Lindsay are twins, right?" Nathan asks. I nod. "Don't you guys have some kind of sixth sense where you know what the other is thinking or feeling?"

I nod. "Yes, sometimes we do."

"Maybe she read your mind," Eric guesses. "Or maybe she noticed your behaviour around Nathan changing."

Eric might be right, but I wasn't completely sure Lindsay knew that way. She couldn't have seen me with Nathan the other night, could she? I was careful about sneaking him in and out of the house. She was in her room the whole time. She couldn't have seen anything.

I'm hyperventilating again. The boys tell me to stay calm. It wasn't easy when all I could think about was what everyone must be saying. Are they going to be talking bad about me?

It takes the guys a couple of tries to get me to breathe normally.

"People can't know about us," I say. "I'm not ready for people to know."

"People are going to find out eventually, Alex," Eric tells me.

"Why would Lindsay do this to me?"

"Well, for one thing she is probably jealous that I like you and not her," Nathan points out.

"Everyone is whispering about me," I say.

Nathan rubs my back. "It's okay, Alex. When you walk out of this room, pretend that you don't see them. Who cares what they say? Let them think what they want. People date all the time. You can't judge someone on who they decide to date. Maybe they won't say anything. Not everyone is going to take it a big deal and care about us dating."

"This is high school, Nathan. Everyone is in your damn business all the time. They are going to want to know what we get up to. Their eyes will be on us. If we were to sleep together, they will know. If we break up, they will know."

Nathan takes my shoulders and makes me look at him. "This may be high school, but it doesn't mean people need to know everything we do. It's no one's business but ours. There's no reason for you to worry, Alex."

Nathan is right. Why am I worrying about it? There was nothing for me to worry about, and it would only make me push Nathan away if I let it get to me.

Eric leaves the room so Nathan and I could have some privacy to talk.

"Alex, listen to me," Nathan says once we are alone. "Everything is going to be alright. I promise." He put his hands on my arms. "You don't need to explain anything to anyone."

I nod. "Okay."

"And please don't confront Lindsay. I know you're angry with her, but I don't want you to do something you might regret. Besides, you know she will deny everything.

She's provoking you. She knows what you're going to do when you figure out it's her."

Nathan is right. I would have to approach her later when we are at home to find out why she would do this to me. Even if I waited until then, it would be pointless. She will deny that she posted about it. I don't even have social media to prove she did it. If I get into a fight with her here, I will be sent to Mr Matthews. He will be pissed to see me in his office. He will either make me see Miss Giovanni, or he may suspend me for real this time for fighting.

I couldn't get suspended for fighting, or for any other act of violence. Mum will kill me.

Nathan kisses me softly when the bell rings. As we leave the classroom, he assures me again that everything was going to be okay.

I hope he is right.

In roll call, I had to do everything I could to avoid looking at my sister. If I saw the smirk, which I know she will give me, I will not be able to control my anger knowing what she wrote online for everyone to see. I still don't understand why she would do that. I would never do that to her, even when I threaten to expose her to Simon for cheating.

Lindsay wasn't the only person I had to avoid looking at. I avoid looking at my classmates also as the anxiety was building up again, terrified of what everyone is thinking about. I keep my eyes on my book as I draw.

I managed to get through the entire day without having another panic attack. Hearing Nathan's words in my head about not worrying about what others say helps me to stay calm. There was one time during the day when Simon approached me in the corridor, making fun of me for being with Nathan. He teased me for only being with him because he had come to my rescue at the party the other night. I ignored Simon and stuck my finger up at him before walking away. Simon knows nothing about how I feel about Nathan.

After school Nathan took me out to the movies, hoping it would take my mind off everything. I doubt it would, but I guess it's worth a try. Now that everyone knew about us, it was okay for us to be seen, even though it made everything awkward with everyone knowing.

"When was the last time you went to the movies?" Nathan asks me as we sit down near the aisle seat in the back of the cinema.

"To tell you the truth, I don't remember. It has been a while." I take a sip of my drink.

"I'm glad you're giving me a chance, Alex. I never thought you would give me one."

I blush, tucking a strand of my hair behind my ear. "I gave you a chance because of the way you spoke to me. There was something in your voice that told me to trust you." I smile. "And I'm glad I gave you a chance."

Nathan returns the smile. He then grabs a handful of his popcorn and stuffs it in my mouth. I whack him in the arm and we both laugh.

Why did I ever think that being in a relationship was bad?

Chapter 23

Some days you wake up thinking everything is going to be okay, not realising how fast your world could come tumbling down. Everything has been going well with Nathan. The hardest part is navigating our relationship, not knowing what people will think. Even if Nathan told me everything was okay, it shouldn't matter what they say.

That Saturday morning was one of those days where I thought nothing would happen. I went out to buy a new sketchbook, as I only had a few pages left. When I return home, I find Nathan's car parked outside our house. We hadn't planned on seeing each other today. So when I saw his car, it surprised me he would show up without telling me.

I headed inside, expecting to see Nathan waiting in the lounge room after Lindsay probably let him in since Mum wasn't home. She and Dereck had an appointment with a wedding planner. But Nathan wasn't in the lounge room when I walked through the front door. Or even the kitchen. Where could he be? He would not have gone up to my room if I wasn't home.

Unless Lindsay told him to go right up there.

There's an uneasy feeling in the pit of my stomach. I run up the stairs. My bedroom door is closed, exactly the way I left it earlier. I open it, stopping short. My heart stops and crumbles to pieces.

Nathan and Lindsay stood in the centre of the room. My sister is wearing a piece of my clothing—denim jeans and a black shirt. Her hair hangs loose around her shoulders with a purple clip-on hair extension piece. She had even taken out her nose ring.

I can't believe this. I know my sister could be a real bitch, but this is a whole new level of bitchiness. We never swap places, even if we are identical. But to see her pretend to be me so she could get her hands on a guy she liked who likes me, how could she think to do that?

The two of them pull apart from my sudden presence. They turn in my direction. Nathan looks between my sister and me, trying to make sense of seeing double. He curses, realising his mistake. How could he not know he wasn't kissing me? Lindsay and I may be identical, but he should know it wasn't me. It's not that hard to tell us apart, even though people still get us mixed up. I mean, I have a purple streak through my hair while Lindsay has a nose ring. We did those things so people could tell us apart.

How could he not see that the purple streak in my sister's hair is an extension?

Lindsay stands there, her mouth open agape. Of course she wasn't expecting me to return home so soon. The bitch thought she could get away with this without me knowing. "Alex."

My heart tightens in my chest. "You bitch!"

I dump my bag on the floor and run out of my room, down the hallway to the stairs.

"Alex, wait!" Nathan calls after me.

I hear his footsteps behind me. I ran down the stairs, almost tripping.

I don't want to talk to Nathan. I don't want to hear his excuses for what he did. There is no explanation for it, except he had lied and said he wanted me, but really he wanted my sister all along. I bet this was all Lindsay's idea. Trick me into thinking that Nathan really does like me and then backstab me later.

I ran out the front door. I don't know where I'm going. All I know is that I needed to get as far away from here as possible. I ran down the street, allowing my feet to take me wherever. Tears fell down my cheeks, blurring my vision. I wipe them just as Nathan catches up with me, grabbing my arm.

I stop and swung my arm at him, slapping him hard in the face. Clenching my teeth together, I shove Nathan hard in the chest, and he lets go of me. My chest feels like it's exploding while my heart feels like it's breaking.

"Get the hell away from me!" I shout at him.

"Let me talk to you, Alex," he begs, catching his breath.

I shake my head. "There's nothing to talk about, Nathan." A lump forms in my throat. "Why don't you go back to Lindsay? She wanted you all along, and she has her wish. She got her hands on you."

Nathan shakes his head. "Alex, no, that's–"

"I never did like you in the first place!" I tell him, not letting him speak until I'm done with what I needed to say. "I don't even know why I went out with you, or why I kissed you. Nor why I even told you about my dad. I shouldn't have done any of that."

Nathan grabs my arms. "I don't want Lindsay! I want you, Alex! And you know very well why you went out with me and kissed me. You like me. You feel something for me. That's why you are with me."

I narrow my eyes at him, shaking him off. "Get your hands off me!"

He listens, letting go of my arms, and steps back. "You need to believe me, Alex. I swear I did not know that was Lindsay back there."

I roll my eyes. That pathetic excuse everyone uses when they can't tell my sister and me apart. "Oh bull crap, Nathan. What do you mean you didn't know that was Lindsay? Lindsay and I are two different people! We're nothing alike! Okay, sure you might have trouble telling us apart, but still you should know which one of us is each! Lindsay has a damn nose piercing while I have a purple streak in my hair. Why is that so hard to tell us apart?"

"I'm sorry. I got confused when she had the purple streak in her hair."

"That was a clip-in hair extension, you jerk! And it's obvious that she took out her piercing!"

"It was just one mistake, Alex. I'm sorry."

I shake my head. "No, Nathan. It wasn't a mistake. Or if it is, I don't care if it is one. The thing is, I trusted you. I can't trust you if you can't tell the difference between my sister and me. How do I know you aren't seeing her behind my back? Now can you understand why I hate people so much? You're nice to them, and then they stab you in the back later. I can't believe you betrayed me."

"Alex, please. I didn't do it on purpose. You can't blame me for not being able to tell you both apart."

I scoff. "Of course I can. If you're going to date identical twins, Nathan, you need to know who is who so you don't want to end up with the wrong twin. It's not that hard to tell us apart when we dress differently so people like you can tell us apart."

"Do you seriously get this upset with everyone who can't tell you and Lindsay apart? Alex, I'm sorry, okay? I swear I did not know that the streak in your sister's hair was a clip. And for her nose ring, I wasn't aware she had taken it out. It must have been the lighting that tricked me. I really thought she was you, Alex!"

I shake my head. I can't believe this. If Mum can tell us apart, who we can never fool, why can't other people do the same? And if Nathan wants to date me, he needs to know how to tell us apart, but it's obvious he can't.

"I don't want to hear any more of your excuses."

"Alex, I–"

I step back from him, holding up my hands to show him I didn't want him to come any closer to me. "Forget it. Just go. You can make Lindsay your girlfriend. You might be better off with her than you are with me. She likes you more than I ever did. In fact, I never liked you anyway. I hate you. I hate my sister. I hate everybody. But I think I hate you more than anyone."

"You can't hate me forever over one mistake," he says.

I frown. Does he not know the kind of person I am by now? "I can, and I will."

I turn to walk away without looking back at him. He calls out to me. I only turn to flip my middle finger up at him. I don't want to see him ever again. And if he tries to chase after me, I'm going to show him where it hurts. I don't need him to make me happy. I'm perfectly fine on my own.

I make my way toward the park. No one is there. Just the other day I was here with Nathan, telling him about my dad. Now it just seems like a total waste of time.

The image of Lindsay sticking her tongue down Nathan's throat is in my head. I can't make it go away. It makes me even angrier just thinking about it. I scrunch my fingers through my hair and pull hard on the roots, letting out a frustrating scream, begging for the images to just go.

I sit under a tree, hugging my knees to my chest and buried my face in my knees, sobbing loudly. I feel so lost. How could I have been such a fool to even realise that Nathan is a great person? He's a jerk like every other guy. None of them are even great. They just come into your life, take what they want before they stab you in the heart. I should have known Lindsay would do something like this. She is an expert at getting what she wants.

Why did I tell Nathan about Dad, about the reason I hated everyone, and show him my drawings? He doesn't even need to know anything about me. I should have kept it all to myself, like I have always done. The concert and the kiss, Nathan was nice there. Why did Lindsay have to come and ruin it all? She already has a boyfriend. She doesn't need to have Nathan too. How can Nathan use the excuse that he couldn't tell us apart? I know we're identical twins, but you're still able to know who is who. He should know that my purple streak is not a freaking clip-in hair extension like the one Lindsay is wearing! She also has a nose ring! I'm sure he could have seen the hole in her nose where the piercing would have been. But according to him, the lighting must have tricked him so he couldn't see where her nose ring was. Bull crap.

Nausea twists around my stomach. I put my hand over my chest, where my heart aches. I have never felt this much pain since my father walked out. This is why I don't get too close to anyone, to prevent myself from this pain.

***

If I could stay out here forever and not return home, I would. But unfortunately I had to return home sometime.

It's late when I get home. The sun has set, and I don't let Mum know I am home. I run up the stairs to my room. But as I enter my room, flashbacks of this afternoon run through my mind. All I can see is Lindsay and Nathan standing in the centre of my room, kissing.

No less than a minute did I get in does Lindsay knock on the door. I'm not going to answer. I don't want to see her. Nor do I ever want to speak to her again. We're done as sisters. She's dead to me. Luckily I'd locked the door, or she would have barged in.

I lie down on my bed, letting my sister's knocks go unanswered.

"Alex, I'm really sorry," she apologies. "Please open the door. Let me talk to you."

Why would she think I would let her talk to me after what she did? There's nothing for us to talk about. She's a bitch. That's what my sister is.

Soon Mum is at my door, wondering what was going on, letting us know if we wanted dinner.

"I don't think Alex is coming down for dinner, Mum," Lindsay tells her.

"Why not?" I hear the concern in Mum's voice. "Is she okay?"

"Something happened between Nathan, Alex and me."

I roll my eyes. She has to tell Mum everything, doesn't she?

I hid my head under the pillow, but it isn't enough to block out the voices. Mum and Lindsay talk like I'm not here.

A soft knock sounds at my door.

"Alex?" Mum calls out to me. "Do you want to talk?"

When she realises I wasn't going to answer her, she walks away. Good. Just leave me alone.

For the rest of the night, Lindsay and Mum constantly came to my door, asking me if I wanted to talk. Even Dereck tries to get me to open the door. Why couldn't anyone see that I didn't want to talk and I just wanted to be left alone?

The next day, the same thing happens again with the constant knocking. Even the phone kept ringing and I knew it was Nathan calling. Besides Lindsay, he was the one person I never wanted to speak to again. I don't care about whatever apology he has; I don't want to hear it.

After a while, I force myself out of bed to do something. I sit at my desk to do my homework, but I couldn't concentrate. I can still picture Nathan and Lindsay. The image wouldn't leave me.

I put on some music. I think of the Hurricane concert and put on their music. Like Nathan had said about their music making him feel better whenever he listens to them, the same went for me once I listened to them more since the concert. The instant their first song that comes up on Spotify on my laptop, the sound of Jason's voice calms me. I sit there, tears in my eyes as I listen. Even with the music playing, I needed something else to calm me.

I need to draw. That should help me feel better. I take out my sketchbook from under my pillow and flip to the last page I had drawn. Nathan's smiling face is staring back at me. The longer I stare at it, the anger rises inside of me as I remember everything we did together. How can everything change with just one blink of an eye?

I let out a piercing scream, ripping the page out and ripping it to pieces. I rip every single drawing I had drawn of him out, letting the tiny pieces of paper fall to the floor of my room.

When I'm done, I sit down on the floor, resting my back up against the bed and cry. Hurricane's music is still playing in the background. I'm such a fool. This is the last time I'm ever going to let a guy fool me into thinking that they like me.

I spot something purple sticking out of my bag. It's the notebook Miss Giovanni had given me. I haven't used it or taken it out of my bag just yet. Something tells me to grab it and write. Would it help me take out the anger I feel, just like Miss Giovanni said it will? Would it be better than drawing?

I crawl across the floor and pull the notebook out of my bag. I grab a blue ink pen from my desk and sit back on the bed. Opening it to the first page, I inhale the scent of the fresh pages of the book. It was like a welcoming feeling, inviting me to write down my emotions and secrets, something that will be kept between me and the pages of this book.

I write today's date and began writing, my hand moving fast along the pages. With the sound of the music playing, it helps me to let the words flow easily. Every lyric Jason sings allows me to express the feelings I felt towards Nathan. Especially with the band reminding me about the concert.

I never believed you could feel your heart actually break into a million pieces. I always thought it was just a description to say how you feel when something tragic happens, losing someone you deeply and truly care about, someone you had trusted with your whole heart. Not until yesterday.

For almost six years I haven't been able to feel any kind of love towards anyone. Hatred was the only thing I could feel. To me, feeling hate was the only thing that made me feel safe from the world, like it was a shield to protect me from getting hurt by others and not getting close to them. Maybe I was too young to feel my heart break when Dad walked out. It only crumbled before from the disappointment of him never coming back. Or maybe that's a totally different situation. I can literally feel my heart breaking in my chest. It makes me feel sick. I feel like a complete fool for trusting this one guy who I thought was different from every other guy, but Nathan is just the same as the others. He's a player who only wants to steal girls' hearts and then crush them to pieces. I let him steal mine. Now there is nothing left of it. There's just a hole, and I have no idea how to fix it.

Why did I like Nathan in the first place? I hate him. I hate everything about him. I hate it when he stalks me like he has nothing better to do. I hate him for stabbing me in the back, mistaking me for Lindsay, who I knew badly wanted him ever since she laid her eyes on him. I mean, I know we're identical twins, but if Nathan knows us well enough, he could actually tell us apart. He should have known it wasn't me he was kissing! I hate Lindsay for liking him. It's like she has nothing else to do with her life besides chasing after guys. I also hate it when Nathan is always right, like he thinks he knows what is actually going through my head. I hate myself for liking him. I hate his gently voice. It's always so calm, like he doesn't yell. I hate his eyes and his smile, like he thinks he has his perfect charm to fool me and to make me fall in love with him, which kind of worked, and I regret it every minute. I hate Nathan for liking me. Out of every girl in the world, why did he have to choose me? What does he even see in me? He may have been a great kisser, but truthfully I hate them. He isn't that great at it like he thinks he is. I hate it when he makes me agree with him, like he knows what I'm really hiding behind the smile I never show. I hate everything about him. I hate him so much, it hurts.

Sometimes the hate I feel towards him hurts so much that I can't breathe from the pain. I just want this feeling to go away. I don't want to feel this way anymore.

I read the words back to myself. It was like a ton of weight was lifted off my shoulders, and it made me feel better, just like Miss Giovanni said it would. But even if I wrote out how I felt, I still felt broken. Like there was nothing left of me. Nathan had gotten me where it hurts.

How do I stop feeling like this?

Chapter 24

I wanted the ground to open up and swallow me whole. It will be so much better than having to walk into English where I have to see both Lindsay and Nathan. I still haven't spoken to any of them, and I'm never planning to. Lindsay may be harder to avoid than Nathan, and Mum isn't pleased I won't talk to her, but I don't care. She is no longer my sister.

I distance myself from them once I get to class, sitting on the other side of the room. Lindsay sits on the other side with a gap in between Nathan, while he sat in his usual spot in front of our teacher's desk. I'm sure Mrs Callea will certainly like the idea of my sister and me not sitting anything near each other; that way we couldn't interrupt her class. And even if my sister wanted to start something, I will only ignore her.

The first thing our teacher did to start the lesson was walk around the classroom, handing out our essays that she had marked over the weekend.

"A lot of you did really well on this essay," she says. "But there are some who still need to improve in some areas. I'm proud of the work you all have done."

Mrs Callea hands back mine. She smiles at me and then walks away. I look down at the essay. The top right-hand corner showed a score of eighty percent in red.

Something made me look up from my paper. When I do, my eyes make contact with Nathan. I immediately felt nauseous when I see him. I quickly turn away and stare down at my paper. A few tears find their way down my cheeks. How could I have been such a fool? I should never have liked Nathan. I wouldn't have to feel this way if I hadn't.

"Alex, is something wrong?" Mrs Callea asks.

Crap. She sees the tears. I quickly wipe my eyes.

"She probably got a very low score. That's why she is crying." Simon laughs.

"Simon, that will be enough, please," Mrs Callea says. "You shouldn't speak because you got a very low score yourself."

Simon doesn't seem to care what our teacher was saying. "Hey, Alex, what did you get on your essay? Zero percent?" He laughs at his own joke.

"That's enough, Simon," Mrs Callea scolds him. "Don't let me warn you again."

That's it. I can't take this anymore. I need to get out of here before I do something I'm going to regret, like punching Simon square in the face. It's something I should do to get him to shut up. Only I stop myself from doing so because he wasn't worth getting expelled or suspended over. I gather up my things. I ignore my teacher when she asks me what I'm doing.

I make my way to the door. Mrs Callea tries to block my way, but I only push past her, walking out of the classroom and head down the corridor. I don't know where I'm going. All I wanted was to get out of here. I'm a fool. I'm sure everyone has heard about Nathan and me breaking up. How long will it be until they tease me about the breakup? Say things like it's my fault we broke up or that I couldn't keep a boyfriend?

Maybe I should just leave and go home. I don't care if I get into trouble for leaving the school grounds. I don't belong here. And if I definitely don't want to see Nathan.

I walk into the nearest girls' toilets before a passing teacher stops to ask what is wrong, or what I'm doing out of class without a hall pass. I don't feel like talking to anyone, nor do I feel like explaining anything.

Thankfully the toilets are empty. I dump my bag on the floor beside the sink. Glancing in the mirror, my reflection greets me back with a horrifying look with red and puffy eyes. I couldn't go back to class. Not looking like this. I turn on the tap and wash my face.

"Alex?" I hear Miss Giovanni's voice coming from outside. "Alex, it's me, Miss Giovanni. Can you come out here so we can talk?"

Damn it. How did she know I was in here? Can't I be left alone for a second?

I don't answer.

"Alex, I know you're in there."

When I didn't respond, she pushes open the door and walks in. I keep my eyes on my reflection. I don't want to turn to her and let her see me like this.

"Go away, please," I tell her. "I really do not feel like talking."

"I think it's best we talk."

I turn to face her, her eyes gentle and filled with concern. "How did you know I was in here?"

"I was walking down the corridor when I saw you running into here. I was just about to come to your class. Your mother called me this morning, saying that she was worried about you. She asked me to talk to you today. Is everything alright?"

No! Nothing is alright! Will everyone just please leave me alone! I don't want to talk about what happened to anyone. No one will understand what I'm going through.

I see the image of Lindsay and Nathan kissing in my mind. It haunts me, and I can't stand to see it anymore. I turn to the wall and kick it a few times, trying to let go of my anger. I expected Miss Giovanni to come over to stop me before I damage something, but she just lets me do whatever I had to do to get rid of my anger. The tears I had managed to stopped, returns. I couldn't hide my emotions any longer. I have to let it go. My life is falling apart.

All because I let Nathan in when I shouldn't.

Miss Giovanni steps towards me and puts a hand on my shoulder. In a gentle voice, she says, "Alex, calm down and tell me what's wrong."

I say the next words without hesitation. "I hate Lindsay! I hate Nathan!"

Miss Giovanni pulls me into a hug. I sob into her chest. "Come back with me to my office and we can talk there. You can tell me why you hate them there."

I follow Miss Giovanni out of the restroom. Once inside her office, she hands me a box of tissues. I thank her and sit down in front of her desk, wiping my eyes.

We sit there in silence for a while. I expected her to say something, encouraging me to spill out everything I'm keeping to myself, but she doesn't. She sits there patiently, waiting for me to talk once I felt ready. Why couldn't everybody be like Miss Giovanni instead of always hassling me to talk?

"Nathan cheated on me with Lindsay," I finally say. "She got him. She has been wanting him for a long time." I tell her everything, remembering clearly what happened. Thinking about it makes my heart crumble more.

Miss Giovanni assures me that everything is going to be fine, but I'm not sure how she could think everything would be fine after what Lindsay did to me. Everything isn't going to be fine. Nothing feels the same after what I witnessed. Nathan is the one person who I had trusted, and now I'm afraid I would never trust him again.

Chapter 25

I spent the morning with Miss Giovanni. If I had any choice at all, I wouldn't have come to school. But even if she had let me stay in her office, I eventually had to go back to class. I don't leave her office until recess. Talking to her made me feel better, but it didn't help with the heartache.

School finally ended for the day after I avoided Nathan and Lindsay the best I could. I rush out of the school grounds, where I didn't bother to wait for my sister. I don't care how she gets home. She can ask Simon for a lift home, or even Nathan since she wants him so desperately. I don't want her in the car with me.

I don't stay home for long. I don't want to be here when Lindsay gets home. Nathan will probably try to call me as well, or maybe he will show up at the house this time. I change out of my uniform, putting on my cap and hiding my face behind my sunglasses, and headed out to the park where I can be alone.

Just as I'm coming out of the house, a car pulls up on the street. I roll my eyes. Of course my sister would ask her stupid boyfriend to drive her home. I'm surprised she didn't ask Nathan.

I walk down the lawn, stopping to stare at them on the footpath. They were making out in the car until Lindsay pushes him off her. As if my sister knew I was standing there, she turns to me, our eyes locking. I see the guilt in her eyes that I never thought I would see on her. She knows what she is doing wrong.

I turn away before any of them get out of the car, making my way down the path towards the park. I couldn't deal with the two of them right now.

Two children are playing in the playground when I get there. Their mother sits on a bench watching them. I sit down at a wooden table, where I watch the two girls for a second. They look to be about seven or eight. Seeing them play happily on the playground reminded me of how close Lindsay and I were at that age. I know I drifted away from everyone after Dad left, but sometimes I wonder why Lindsay and I grew apart. Maybe it was because I pushed her away, not wanting to tell her how I felt. She would have felt the same way about Dad leaving. I'm such a horrible sister. We should never have drifted apart, but Dad was the one who tore the family apart when he left.

I turn away from the sisters and open my sketchbook. The moment I put my pencil to paper, it relaxes me, keeping my mind off everything. I stay at the park until the sun sets. When I can no longer see what I'm drawing as it gets darker, I closed my book and just sit there. I don't care how dark it gets. I don't want to go home.

I hear footsteps approaching on the grass. I don't look up to see who it is. They stand beside me and I know it's Lindsay without looking in her direction. She stands there in silence before she speaks.

"Mum wanted me to come and get you," she says. "Dinner is ready."

"Tell her I'm not hungry," I reply without looking at her.

"You still like him, don't you?"

My head shot up at her. I take off my sunglasses and place them on top of my cap. "What? No! Why would I like that moron after you put your dirty hands all over him?"

"Nathan is not a moron."

"Of course he is. All guys are." *Some are. Nathan wasn't, but now I don't know.*

I stare back down at my book. I can see her staring at me from the corner of my eye. Seriously, but doesn't she have anything else to do besides stare at me? Like head back home to Mum?

"Nathan may be a moron," Lindsay says, "but I still think you like him. You're just upset at the moment to even realise that your feelings for him are still there."

I look up at her, narrowing my eyes. How would she know how I even feel about him? She doesn't know how

I feel. "For crying out loud, why do you just assume I like him? I hate him, okay? I hate him!"

I stand up, grabbing my book and push my sister out of the way to head home. What does Lindsay know about how I feel?

"Why do you keep on running away every time someone wants to know something?" Lindsay hurries after me. "Or when they try to help you?"

"It's because it is no one's business who I like and who I don't like. I also don't need help from anyone."

"Can you please stop walking so I can talk to you, Alex?"

I let out a frustrated sigh. Why should I stop and talk to her? I don't want to listen to whatever she has to say. Not if she is going to keep on questioning me whether I like Nathan. I don't want to like him or any guy. I'm not going to fall in love with anyone. And I'm never going to forgive my sister for what she did. I can't help but wonder what Lindsay was even thinking when she was making out with Simon in the car earlier. Didn't she feel bad after she two-timed him for Nathan?

I stop and turn to her, hoping she will stop firing the same question at me repeatedly. If she does, I'm out of here.

"Look, I just want to let you know I broke up with Simon this afternoon," Lindsay tells me. "I felt horrible for what I did to you and Nathan that I couldn't stand to face Simon after what I did. And I should have broken up with him a long time ago. I had wanted to break up with him for a while, but I was scared. I didn't want to be missing out on anything, so I stayed with him. That's why I have been sneaking around with other guys because I didn't know how to let go of Simon. I was searching for someone to make me happy. Simon made me happy, but after a while he made me feel like crap, especially when he spoke about you. Sure, I complained to him about you all the time, but he would always say nasty stuff about you that I didn't like. I should have said something, but sometimes I was so angry with you that I agreed with whatever he said. But now I realise that not only was I hurting you because of how selfishly I wanted Nathan, but I was also hurting myself with what I was doing to you."

Wow. Lindsay actually had a conscience. Since when does she care how I feel?

She goes on. "I knew what I did was wrong, and I was glad when you walked in to stop me from doing anything else."

I want to say something, but I don't. I'm not sure if Lindsay is truly sorry for what she said, but this is the first time she is actually apologising for something she has done to me. So instead of saying anything, I allowed her to keep speaking while I listened.

"I know you truly hate me right now, and I don't blame you," Lindsay tells me. "I just want you to hear me out before you judge me or say something nasty that I'm sure

I deserved to be called. I miss having you around as my sister, Alex. I miss when we would talk about girl stuff. The day Dad walked out, you turned your back on me. You aren't the only one who was hurt when Dad left, but it hurt more when you didn't want me around, especially when we were going through the same thing. I know I have tormented you about everything. Trying to get you to like what I like, but I have always thought you were some kind of freak, not knowing the real reason you hated everything. I'm really sorry for what I did to you. And just so you know, I'm always going to be there if you ever want to talk about anything. About Dad or Nathan, I don't care. I will listen."

I slip my hands into the pockets of my jeans. For all these years I have never really thought about how selfish I have been. Instead of going through the same thing together when Dad left, I wanted to go at it on my own. My sister was hurting also, and I pushed her away to focus on myself. "I miss you too, Lindsay."

Lindsay smiles at me. "Well then, let's talk now." Her smile fades. "I'm sorry for what I did, but don't blame Nathan. It's my entire fault. I was jealous that he liked you and not me. I don't know why I wanted him when I already had Simon. Now I have no one. Dressing like you was the only way he would look at me. I knew posing as you was wrong, and I regret it. I'm glad you walked in when you did."

She looks away from me for a moment before turning back to me. "I'm also sorry I told your secret about you being with Nathan. It was Emilynn's idea to spread it on Facebook. We..." she stammers. "We told everyone in our grade that you two were dating. Everyone was shocked at first, but they thought you two made a perfect couple. Looking at you, I can tell you still like him, even if you're trying to hide your feelings. You can deny everything about what you may think about Nathan, but as your sister I know you still like him. Seeing you with him, I swear I don't even remember the last time you were happy, and I'm glad you have found someone. But now, because of me, I had ruined everything for you. I'm sorry, Alex."

I blush, thinking about Nathan. I wanted to feel all the anger in my body right now, but all I could feel was my heart breaking. How can I still have feelings for him? I don't like him anymore.

I think about the kisses we shared, the concert we attended, and the fun we had at Splash Resort. I may miss that, but I still hated him as much as I hated everyone else. Since talking to Nathan, telling him my secret and the problems I had, he had changed my thinking, making sure that I wouldn't go back to loathing anyone. Out of every guy I have come across, Nathan was the only one who has helped me. He said things like telling me how beautiful I look and meant it. I got butterflies whenever I was around him. I never felt the way I did with anyone, even if they were to say nice things to me. There was just something about Nathan that made me fall for him. I can't explain it. It just happened. He brought the walls I had put up to protect myself down. He helped me to see things I never saw in myself before.

Maybe Lindsay is right. Maybe I do still like him, even with how much he had hurt me.

"How do you know if I still like him?" I ask.

Lindsay gives me a guilty look. "Please don't hate me, but you dropped your notebook in class this morning when you stormed out. I shouldn't have read what you wrote, but I did. I really wish you could have spoken to me about everything you have been going through. We are sisters, Alex. Twins. When one of us is hurting, the other one feels it too. I'm really sorry about being a jerk to you. Alex, you have been hiding your feelings since Dad left. Mum and I have been trying to get you to open up to us for years, but you never wanted us to be there for you. You don't want anyone in your life. And then Nathan comes along and you tell him everything that you never wanted Mum or me to know. It hurts that you told him everything first and not me, but I'm glad you told someone. Never think it's wrong to talk to someone about what's bothering you. There is nothing wrong with telling anyone how you feel."

My sister is right. I know I shouldn't hate Nathan for failing to tell my sister and me apart. Lindsay was the one who fooled him. What right did I have to accuse him for not knowing when so many people can't tell us apart? I think about how I opened up to him, telling him things about my dad. If I could open up to him, I could do the same thing to my sister and Mum. They needed to know about it more than anyone else should. The three of us have all gone through the same thing. Why did I push Mum and my sister away? I can't keep hiding my feelings from them forever.

And as much as I wasn't happy with Lindsay reading my notebook, I shouldn't have to let her find out the way she did through the book. Maybe none of this would have ever happened. Maybe Lindsay wouldn't have gone after Nathan if we had been closed.

But right now, I was still unsure how I was supposed to feel about Nathan.

"I don't know how I feel about Nathan right now," I say. "I don't know if I want to be with him. But there is something I should have told you long before I drifted away from you and Mum."

I tell her everything that I told Nathan about Dad and the reasons I turned against everyone.

Chapter 26

Telling Lindsay everything lifted a weight off my shoulders. For once, we didn't argue. We just talked and listened to what each other had to say. We take our time walking home. Before we entered the house, I hugged her. It was the first hug we had given each other since we were twelve. It felt good to have my sister's arms wrapped around me.

As I enter our house, I realise then that it wasn't just my sister I needed to talk with. I also needed to talk with Mum and Dereck as well before I could even decide what I wanted to do with Nathan. Dereck was over for dinner again. As the four of us sit down to eat, I watch Dereck and my mother carefully. Is it selfish for me to hate on a man, afraid of what he could do to my mother just because my father did it? Dereck may never end up being like Dad. When he is around Mum, he always makes her happy. Before Mum met Dereck, she was never happy until she started dating him. He brought the happiness she lost when Dad walked out on us and helped Mum to fall in love again.

Just how Nathan has made me feel for the past week, helping me to realise that there was nothing wrong with falling in love. Miss Giovanni had told me I needed to not let the emotions I felt towards my dad hold me back from doing things I wanted to do. It was the same with how I felt towards anyone else.

And I knew I needed to give Dereck a chance to show that he wasn't going to be anything like Dad.

After dinner, I told Mum I wanted to talk to her. I needed to talk to her first before I could talk with Dereck. Leaving him and my sister to do the dishes, Mum and I sit in the lounge room on the couch.

I spill everything to my mother about what I had told my sister. I told her I was sorry for everything, with the way I had been treating her.

Mum rests a hand on my shoulder and smiles. "It's okay, Alex. It really is. Expressing how you felt hasn't been easy, especially with what your father did. In fact, there's something I need to give you. Something I should have given to you a long time ago, but I didn't think you were ready to process it. You sister has already gotten hers, and I think now would be a good time for you to have yours."

Mum gets off the couch and tells me she'll be back in a second, heading upstairs.

Lindsay walks into the lounge room and smiles. "How's it going?"

I return a smile. "Okay. Mum said she is just getting something."

Lindsay bites her lip, as if she knew what Mum was getting, and sits down on an armchair across from me. "You don't mind if I stay here with you for this?"

"What is Mum getting?"

"Something that will explain everything about why Dad left."

I agreed to let my sister stay. Mum comes down a few minutes later with an envelope in her hand. She hands it to me before sitting down next to me.

I hold it in my hands, my name scribbled on the envelope in Dad's messy handwriting.

"You don't have to read this now," Mum tells me. "You can read it whenever you want. Your father wrote both of you girls a letter about why he left."

I stare at it, wondering if I even wanted to read it. For a long time I have wanted to know why he had left, and if I was the blame for him leaving. Now was my chance to find out.

I open the letter carefully and read it silently to myself.

Dear Alex,

By the time you read this letter, I will be long gone. You'll probably have so many questions about why I left. Alex, I want you to know that I love you and your sister so much. You both mean the world to me, but I need to leave.

I want you to know that you aren't the reason I left. Never blame yourself for that. I never planned on becoming a father. Not until I first held you in my arms. Your mother and I got together because of a one-night stand, never planning to see each other again until she learned she was pregnant. I stayed to help raise you and Lindsay. But when it came close to your twelfth birthday, I realised I needed to leave.

It's hard to explain to you about everything, things that I'm not even sure you will understand. Maybe someday in the future you will understand better, and your mother can explain more to you about why I left you girls.
Happy birthday, Alex.
Love Dad

I stare at the letter in my hand, unsure what I was supposed to make of it. Dad didn't leave because I did something wrong. He left because he needed to. And even though he said he loved me, he never planned to be a father to Lindsay and me. The man I looked up to didn't really care about me.

I look up at Mum and Lindsay as they watch me. From the kitchen/lounge room doorframe, Dereck stands there quietly, watching me carefully. I replay Dad's words from the letter. He didn't want me. The jerk never wanted me. He only stayed because Mum was pregnant and then left once we were twelve because he thought it was time for him to leave.

Scrunching the letter in my hand, I throw my arms around my mother and bury my face on her shoulder as I sob. She rubs her hand up and down my back to soothe me. Lindsay joins us and wraps her arms around me from behind.

"Dad didn't want us," I choke out.

"No, he didn't, Alex," Mum says. "Your father and I met at a club, had a one-night stand, and we weren't planning to see each other again. Though part of me wanted to see him again, and I did once I found I was pregnant with you girls. He could have walked away, left me to raise you both on my own, but he decided to stay. We got married, and we found out we were having twins. He was thrilled about becoming a father. But I guess I was wrong about his happiness. He had planned to leave once you girls had gotten to a certain age. He didn't love me, and only married me because he felt obligated to. I didn't know how he really felt until your twelfth birthday. I'm sorry you girls have to go through this."

"It's okay, Mum," Lindsay says. "We love you."

"I love you both too."

I hug my mother closely, wondering how I could say so many horrible things to her over the years about Dad leaving, only to find out that Dad never even loved us? How can you feel obligated to be with someone? The hope of Dad returning was gone. Mum and Lindsay were right. Dad was never coming back. And for these past six years, I have been a horrible person to everyone, putting the blame on them for my anger with dad leaving. All this time I figured I had done something wrong for him to leave, but it wasn't me. It was Dad who didn't love any of us, even if he said he loved me in the letter. If he loves me, why did he leave? All because he wasn't planning on becoming a father?

I push Mum and my sister off me and sit there, still holding onto Dad's letter in my hand. I stare at it before ripping it up into a million pieces, letting out a frustrated scream.

"I hate you!" I scream. Throwing the paper in the air, it falls like confetti around me. I grab the envelope next, screaming "I hate you" repeatedly until I cover my face with my hands and cry.

I sob against my mother's arm. She put her arms around me.

"It's okay, Alex," she whispers.

"I hate Dad," I tell her. "Why did he have to leave?"

"Shh, it's okay. We don't have to talk about this right now. Why don't you calm down, and maybe tomorrow we can talk more about this?"

I nod, but I don't move from my spot.

"I will take her up to her room," Dereck says.

Instead of protesting about him taking me, I let Dereck pick me up from the couch. Carefully he carries me out of the lounge room and up the stairs to my room. I rest my head on his shoulder, sobbing quietly. Being in his arms reminded me of the days when Dad used to carry me. Especially when I may have fallen asleep in the car and he would carry me up to my room to put me to bed.

Dereck reaches for the light switch and then lies me down on my bed.

"There you go, Alex," he tells me.

"Thank you, Dereck."

His eyes widened from my words. He gives me a small smile before he turns to leave.

"Dereck?" I sit up.

He turns back to me. "Yes?"

I stand up and hug him. This startles him and at first it was like he wasn't sure what he should do, hesitating for a moment before placing his arms around me.

"Thank you, Dereck for being there for my mum," I tell him. "I'm sorry for the way I have treated you."

"It's okay," he says. "I understand what you are going through, Alex. But I want you to know that I will never replace your father."

I pull away from him. "I will go to the art exhibition with you next month."

Dereck smiles. "I look forward to going to it with you."

I hug him one last time before he leaves my room.

I curl up on my bed. Now the person I needed to make amends with is Nathan, and I have no idea how I'm going to do that.

Chapter 27

They say love is about taking a risk. Sometimes it lasts, sometimes it doesn't.

I think about Dad's letter, memorising every word about what he had said. Mum took a risk to fall in love with him, only he didn't return the love. He just married her because he felt obligated to be with her, all because he'd accidentally gotten her pregnant. He had a choice to leave, but stayed with her. Dad waited until Lindsay and I had gotten to a certain age, then left. Didn't even say goodbye, just left us a letter because he was too much of a coward to say it to our faces that he didn't even care about us.

How could I have not seen the signs early on that Dad didn't love us? That at some point in our lives, he was going to leave us all? For the past few years, I believed that maybe I had done something to make Dad leave. Now I know it wasn't me.

What if Nathan were to do the same thing? What if he loved me for a short time and then left me when he felt like we shouldn't be together anymore? I want to be with him eternally. I don't want to be left heartbroken like my mother was when Dad left. How do I handle another heartache after what Dad did if I were to lose Nathan? After Lindsay had explained her side of the story, my heart didn't feel like it's broken anymore. Just a sinking feeling of sadness about what a fool I have been all these years to believe Dad would someday come home.

Nathan is a nice guy. He didn't care what issues I was facing, or why I hated him. He just worked around me and made me change my mind about him. Every other guy would have just kept their distance from me. Not Nathan Bridges. He showed how he cared. When he said I was beautiful, he meant it. He never joked about it. He showed me he cared by looking me straight in the eye. Nathan liked me even if I didn't show him how I felt.

How is it possible to hate someone so much, and still somehow fall in love with them?

Nathan doesn't deserve the way I have been treating him. And I had no right to treat him poorly because he couldn't tell Lindsay and me apart. Many people couldn't tell us apart.

I know what I needed to do. Even though I'm terrified about getting hurt by Nathan, I needed to take a risk. People come and go, but only the people who truly care about you will stay. Dad may not care about me, but at least I had Mum and Lindsay. Dereck also, who I needed to give a chance to prove he will never be like Dad.

And Nathan was another person who was here with me. I hope he takes me back.

Taking out my notebook, I write every emotion I was feeling. Perhaps someday I will show this to Miss Giovanni. I decide to write a letter to Dad, one that I will never send. I let out the emotions I had kept in me for the past six years, things I wanted to say to him but will never get to.

When I finish writing the letter, every piece of anger I had was gone. Talking with Lindsay, Mum and Dereck has helped me to see that everything is okay, that I didn't need to be angry with the world. Especially with the one person who made me feel that way. Mum had already informed me earlier that she was going to let Miss Giovanni know to see me. She was someone I knew I could talk to about this, and maybe help me move on, to get past the truth about my dad.

Maybe I could even enter that art competition Mrs Hawkins wants me to. Even though I kept my drawings private about my dad, maybe I could do a piece of artwork to express how I deeply feel about him.

But right now, I needed to tell Nathan how I felt.

I get to school early the next morning, wanting to speak to Nathan first thing before class starts. I sit near the library like I do every morning, hoping Nathan will come by. As I wait for him to arrive, I thought of what I'm going to say to him. Would he accept my apology for the way I've treated him? Would he even want to still like me?

I snap myself out of my thoughts when I sense Nathan's presence. I look up as I see him walking by me, not glancing my way. My stomach does a somersault when I see him. Hopefully it won't be too late to tell him that I'm sorry about everything.

"Nathan," I call out to him as I stand up from the seat.

Nathan stops. He stands there, hesitating for a moment before looking my way. His eyes are weary, as if he hadn't gotten a wink of sleep in days. My stomach twists. Did I make him do that?

"Alex. Hi."

"Can I please talk to you?"

He nods, and we walk inside the building and into an empty classroom. He watches me, which makes me feel even more nervous than before.

"This isn't about the other day is it, Alex?" Nathan says. "If it is, I said–"

"Lindsay explained everything to me." I take a deep breath and exhale slowly. I can tell him this. If I could express how I felt with Lindsay and Mum, I can do it with Nathan too. "I'm sorry if I didn't believe you. I should have known you wouldn't betray me like that. I feel like such a fool."

Nathan puts his bag down on the table and takes a step towards me. "You aren't a fool, Alex. You have every right to be mad at me. I'm the one who is a fool. I got tricked into thinking it was you. I did not realise it was Lindsay at all. She acted like you so well."

I shake my head. "No. I shouldn't have given you a hard time for not being able to tell us apart. Maybe before I got this streak in my hair, you wouldn't have been able to. Lindsay and I can fool so many people with our appearances. The only person who can really tell us apart is our mum. She somehow always knew who was who. We can never fool her. I got this streak so it couldn't confuse people with who we are, and Lindsay got a rose ring. But even then people still can't tell us apart."

He chuckles. "People often get my brother and me mixed up sometimes, and we aren't even twins."

I couldn't help but laugh at that. I then reach over and stroke his cheek. "Nathan, please forgive me. I don't hate you at all. I like you. Really like you."

Nathan smiles. "I like you too."

He grabs my hand that is resting on his cheek and holds it before leaning forward and brushes his lips against mine.

As I kiss him, I promise myself I will never dislike someone again. Never will I let someone hold back my emotions or turn against anyone again.

But what I do hate about Nathan Bridges is how he opened my heart. And I'm thankful he did.

Epilogue

Five months later

Take deep breaths, Alex, I tell myself. *You can do this. Everything is going to work out fine.*

The art gallery will open to the public soon. I bite my fingernails, still not believing I let Mrs Hawkins talk me into entering the art competition. There were several other art students from other schools that entered tonight, and I have no idea how my work will compare to others. Mrs Hawkins is the only one who has seen my artwork, and I have no idea how everyone else will react tonight. Especially Lindsay and Mum. Even with after coming to terms with myself that Dad was never coming back after reading that letter, I still haven't shown them my artwork. Tonight will be the first time they will get to see any of it.

In the last few months since getting to know Dereck, we have been visiting art galleries together. I try not to think too much about Dad when we visited them, telling myself that Dad walked away and it was up to me to move on. Mum and Dereck were getting married in just a few weeks. As much as it was hard for me to accept Dereck, I was trying my best to see the good side of him, and how he has made my mother feel since the divorce. Going to the art gallery with him helped a lot with my inspiration and I'm glad I agreed to go with Dereck.

Spending time with him and thinking about my dad has helped me decided on the art project I wanted to do for the competition.

Mrs Hawkins walks over to me, handing me a paper cup with water. "How are you feeling, Alex?"

"Nervous." I take the cup from her. "What if no one likes the painting?"

My teacher gives me an assuring smile. "Alex, you don't need to worry. Your painting is going to wow everyone in the room. It may not win first place, but at least you gave this art competition a go."

I return a smile. "Thank you, Mrs Hawkins, for believing me in this competition."

"You're welcome, Alex. So, this is what's going to happen. People are going to go around and glance at everyone's artwork. Among the crowd will be the judges, and at the end of the night they will announce the first three winners. And don't worry if you don't win first place or any of the first three places, just remember that you did a great job with your work."

For the past few months, I have been spending my lunch and sometimes afternoons working on my project. Only Mrs Hawkins has seen me working on it. I wouldn't allow Lindsay or Nathan to come see me while I am in the art room.

Now they were all about to see it, and I have no idea how they will react.

The doors soon open to the gallery. Gulping down the water, I look out for my family, my boyfriend, and of course Miss Giovanni. Nathan is the first person I spotted. He makes his way over to me and wraps me in a hug, and kisses me. He then looks up at the painting, his eyes widening.

"Wow, this is incredible," he tells me. "The best that I have seen since you first showed me your sketchbook."

"Thanks, Nathan. Have you seen Mum and Lindsay? I'm nervous about what they are going to think."

Nathan put an arm around my waist. "Don't be nervous. They are going to love it just as much as I do. I saw them outside. They should be here soon."

I keep a look out for them. I soon spot Lindsay, and she hurries over to me, wrapping her arms around me. Dereck and Mum walk over, hand-in-hand. Behind them is Miss Giovanni.

"I'm so proud of you, Alex," Lindsay tells me. For the past few months, we have been trying to prepare our relationship. It was slow, and since getting rid of Simon in her life, she has been a much better person, and even took a break from dating. We tried to make time for each other, to listen to what was on our minds, and to spend some time together like we used to.

"Thanks, Linds."

Mum is a few metres from me when she stops to look at the painting. She gasps at it, and I twist my bracelets around my wrists as I wait for her to say something about it all. She and Dereck walk the rest of the way over to me.

"Alex, this painting is wonderful," Mum tells me as she stands beside me.

We glance up at the painting. In my sketchbook, I often just sketch a picture. I never used colour besides a pencil, sometimes charcoal. This time for the art competition I used paint. It was a painting of Dad where he was holding me when I was a newborn. This painting was my way of finally letting him go. I wanted to capture the first love in a father and daughter relationship. Whether Dad said he loved me and Lindsay, when I see this picture, I want to believe he really did. Even if I will never know the real reason he left and no longer wanted the responsibility of my sister and me, I wanted this picture to differ from all the drawings I have made of Dad.

Letting go of Dad hasn't been easy. Sometimes I still think about him, wishing I could go back to the time of my twelfth birthday, to stop him from leaving. But as I spend time with Nathan, my sister and my mum, I realise that sometimes you can't hold on to the past. There's always a memory that will take you back, but you couldn't let that moment take over your whole life and stop you from moving forward. With the help of Nathan, my family, and Miss Giovanni, I have been trying my best to make minor changes for myself. Like taking a step to try out this art competition to put my work on display. In the past, I wouldn't have agreed to do that, afraid of what people thought of my work. I even started my own Instagram account to showcase my artwork. Mrs Hawkins is even helping me look into courses I could do next year for university to develop my art skills, and Miss Giovanni has been helping to prepare with applying for the courses.

"Alex, this is wonderful," Mum tells me.

I smile. "I was afraid of what you were going to say since it was a picture of Dad."

Mum returns a smile, letting go of Dereck's hand and pulling me into a hug. "I'm so proud of you. This is an amazing painting."

"If Dad were here, do you think he would love the painting?"

Mum pulls away and rests her hands on my shoulders. Though she was proud of me, there was a mixture of sadness in her eyes from my comment. "Of course he would. He would have been proud. Sometimes I wished he could have stayed to see the achievements you girls make in your lives. But even if he isn't here, I'm proud of what you have done for yourself, Alex."

"Thanks, Mum."

Dereck hugs me next. "I'm proud of you, too, Alex. And thank you for inviting me, allowing me to be a part of this."

I smile at him. "And thank you for inviting me to those art exhibitions. It has been a great inspiration for me, and I couldn't have done that without you."

Miss Giovanni steps forward, shaking my hand. "Well done, Alex. This is amazing. Something completely different from your drawings. You're going to grow into a fine artist someday."

Mrs Hawkins comes over to us, where she had come back from talking to someone. She chats with my mother about my artwork and praises me for my hard work. She then gets a picture with all of us in it to remember this night.

As Nathan puts an arm around my waist, Lindsay puts an arm around my shoulders, Mum and Dereck standing behind me, I realise just how important I am with having them in my life. If I had hated them, I wouldn't have any of them standing here with me right now, supporting something I love and am proud of.

Even if Dad had walked out of my life, I still had these amazing people, and I never want to change that.

Acknowledgements

I can't tell you how happy I am to have this book finally out there. It almost felt like I could never publish it. I have been working on this story on and off since I began writing it when I was sixteen or seventeen. It's one of my favourite books I have written, and probably the only book I wrote in my teens that I kept working on to publish it someday.

There were times when I felt like this story would never be good enough to publish. I mean, my writing style from my teens is definitely different from my writing style in my thirties. There is so much I have learned about writing since then, which is what made it so much harder to work on this story. Like, for a while I felt that my writing was too immature, and I wasn't able to rewrite this story, but Alex Jennings was always at the back of my mind. She was a character I could never stop thinking about. Especially whenever I listened to Lindsay Lohan's song *Confessions of a Broken Heart*, which was a huge inspiration to Alex's story. Or even when I listen to Simple Plan's songs *Perfect* or *Problem Child*, it always makes me think about Alex.

Let alone the sequel I wrote, but I don't think I'm going to publish that one. I don't know if I ever will, but maybe someday when the time is right, I will go back to it. Even if I never go back to the sequel, I always enjoyed this story about Alex.

The first person I want to thank is my friend Jamie-Lee Wilcock. Jamie, you have been a great friend to me in high school, and you were one of the first people I had shown this story to in its early stages of writing. You gave me tips on what to write and how you pictured Alex's appearance, even though I never really agreed to make her Gothic as I couldn't picture her as that, but perhaps that could have worked for Alex too.

Thank you to Sarah Hitchcock for picking out this book on the old story platform we used to write on before Wattpad, and helping me on ways to improve this story.

Thank you to Sarah Swartz for your endless support on this story.

And lastly, I would like to thank Simple Plan. You were the inspiration for Hurricane (though in the first draft I used you as the band in the story, but changed it in later drafts). I have been listening to you guys since I was sixteen. You have been the band who always made me feel good about myself, and over the years you have shown me where I belong.

About the Author

Jessica Madden was born and raised in Sydney, Australia. She began writing stories since the age of eight. When she was nine, she realised that she wanted to be a writer more than anything in the world. At twenty-three years old, Jessica published her first book *Right Here Waiting for You*. Writing about characters falling in love has always been her favourite thing to write about.

When she is not writing, Jessica is often daydreaming up new storylines, and can be found lost in reading a good book.

You can follow her on Instagram, Threads and X @JessicaCMadden

Also by Jessica Madden

YOUNG ADULT FICTION

Right Here Waiting For You
The Jet Lag Diaries
Silent Love
If You Had Stayed
Hating Jamie Jackson
This Song Is For You

Storm Chasers
Chasing the Storm
Chasing Tornadoes

I Wasn't Supposed To Fall For You
I Wasn't Supposed To Fall For You
It's All Because Of You

NEW ADULT FICTION

With You
One Whole Night with You
Every Moment with You

Maisy Grove Weddings
The Art of Moving On

WHAT I HATE ABOUT YOU

The Art of Faking It (coming soon)